2009

'That boy must be about ten years old,' he said. 'Would that be right?'

Nell nodded, unable to utter a word. Joel continued to look at her, as though he were stripping her naked and looking through to her soul as well.

'Is he my son?'

Again she nodded, looking down at her clasped hands in her lap. 'Yes.' The word came out in a whisper.

Rebecca Lang trained to be a State Registered Nurse in Kent, England, where she was born. Her main focus of interest became operating theatre work, and she gained extensive experience in all types of surgery on both sides of the Atlantic. Now living in Toronto, Canada, she is married to a Canadian pathologist and has three children. When not writing, Rebecca enjoys gardening, reading, theatre, exploring new places, and anything to do with the study of people.

Recent titles by the same author:

THE BABY SPECIALIST
CHALLENGING DR BLAKE
A BABY FOR JOSEY

DONCASTER LIBRARY AND INFORMATION SERVICE	
30122021435975	
Askews	11-Nov-2004
ROMANCE	£13.00
LP	

THE SURGEON'S SECRET SON

BY
REBECCA LANG

All the characters in this book have no existence outside the imagination of the author, and have no relation whatsoever to anyone bearing the same name or names. They are not even distantly inspired by any individual known or unknown to the author, and all the incidents are pure invention.

All Rights Reserved including the right of reproduction in whole or in part in any form. This edition is published by arrangement with Harlequin Enterprises II B.V. The text of this publication or any part thereof may not be reproduced or transmitted in any form or by any means, electronic or mechanical, including photocopying, recording, storage in an information retrieval system, or otherwise, without the written permission of the publisher.

MILLS & BOON and
MILLS & BOON with the Rose Device
are registered trademarks of the publisher.

First published in Great Britain 2004
Large Print edition 2004
Harlequin Mills & Boon Limited,
Eton House, 18-24 Paradise Road,
Richmond, Surrey TW9 1SR

© Rebecca Lang 2004

ISBN 0 263 18174 X

Set in Times Roman 17 on 18½ pt.
17-1104-45952

Printed and bound in Great Britain
by Antony Rowe Ltd, Chippenham, Wiltshire

CHAPTER ONE

NELL MONTAGUE MD eased her car into one of the last available spots in the staff parking lot at Gresham General Hospital, Gresham, Ontario, and turned off the engine with a satisfied sigh. At this rate she would be on time for the international symposium on plastic surgery and burns that was to be held at the convention centre over on the next street from the hospital, a comfortable walk on this pleasant sunny day in early June.

First checking her appearance quickly in the rear-view mirror, she gathered up her briefcase and a sheaf of papers, mostly yesterday's mail, which she had not had time to read, about the upcoming conference. There would be time for her to get a cup of coffee after she had registered for the meeting, then quickly go through the papers at the last minute.

The walk in the sunshine was a welcome respite in a life that seemed more and more to be governed by the clock these days. She thrived on it all, she knew that. She rose to the challenge and liked the adrenaline rush that it all gave her. The main stress in her job was in finding enough time for her son, Alec, forcing time. Sometimes that stress overshadowed the other source of regret that had hung over her for the last nine years, had never really left her…

Briskly she thrust those thoughts out of her mind, something that was not hard to do on such a lovely day, not like those bleak days in the dead of winter that invited introspection. For a few minutes she felt totally free as she walked, recapturing something of her early youth, knowing that she looked attractive in her simple oyster-coloured linen trouser suit and the rose-coloured silk sleeveless blouse underneath, well suited to the heat of early summer. Usually she gave little thought to her appearance, garbed as she was for most of the time in the ubiquitous green or blue scrub suit and white lab coat, then covered up even more for the operating rooms. Her newly washed hair, light brown streaked with blonde, blew around her face in the breeze.

Ah, life was good when one could take pleasure in simple things. She even revelled in walking in shoes that had relatively high heels, which made her feel feminine, instead of the surgical clogs or rubber boots that she galumphed around in during surgery in the operating suite of the burns unit in the hospital.

The conference centre was an imposing high-rise building of glass, steel and concrete, right in the heart of the city, and as Nell pushed her way through the revolving glass doors into the vast marble tiled lobby she was greeted by several colleagues from among the milling crowd.

'Hi!' She waved and smiled at them, striding out to the registration desk. When that was done, she got herself a cup of coffee from one of the tables set up for the purpose and then in a relatively quite corner she slit open the mail that had come recently about the meeting, listing any changes in the programme. Sometimes a week would go by before she had a chance to read her mail, leaving it to the weekend.

There were so many interesting lectures and workshops to go to that making a choice about which ones to attend had been difficult. Idly, she checked those for which she had registered, looking for any changes. The first one was to start in a few minutes, at nine o'clock.

Then she felt as though time stood still, that her surroundings had floated away out of conscious awareness, as a name jumped out at her, a name of a replacement lecturer for the first talk.

'Oh, my heavens!' she said aloud. 'It can't be, surely?' Glancing around surreptitiously, she saw that no one was within immediate earshot. Her heart seemed to do a little jump, stop for a second or two, and then start up again with a deep, sonorous pounding as she stared at the name. The talk was to be about some of the latest surgical techniques in the treatment of severe burns.

Joel Matheson…there was the name in solid print. Nell stared at it as though it might dissolve in front of her eyes. After all those years, ten years, he had suddenly, unexpectedly surfaced, engendering in her a feeling of something like panic, her previous sang-froid disappearing like the proverbial mist before the sun, putting her back into the mind-set of a sixteen-year-old girl, as she had been when she had first met Dr Joel Matheson.

How very odd it seemed that she had spent a long time looking for him, then when she had more or less given up an active search, he should suddenly materialize without any effort on her part. She swallowed, her throat constricted by such powerful emotion that she thought she might faint.

The original lecturer, she read numbly, had been taken ill and had been replaced by Dr Joel Matheson of Montreal, who had kindly agreed to do it at very short notice.

'Hey, Nell, are you going to the first surgical lecture?' One of her colleagues, Dr Trixie Deerborne, accosted her in the hall, and she looked up blankly.

Trixie was a bubbly, chatty person, sometimes too chatty, very focussed on herself so that she was not likely to pick up on the blank look of shock that was on her own face, Nell hoped as she strove to reply.

'I...um...yes,' she managed to get out, as Trixie sat down beside her on the bench.

Trixie, more astute than usual, stared at her. 'Hey, are you OK?' she asked. 'You look a little green around the gills.'

'I'm all right,' Nell mumbled. And not wishing to appear mysterious with her colleague, who could keep a confidence, she pointed at Joel Matheson's name and added, 'The first speaker has been replaced by Dr Joel Matheson. I used to know him.'

'Ah,' Trixie said, looking at her with uncharacteristic comprehension. 'A light dawns. He used to mean something to you, right?'

'You could say that,' Nell said quietly. That was the biggest understatement she had made in her life.

'Come on, then,' Trixie said, 'otherwise we won't get a decent seat. You might as well bite the bullet and give him the once-over.'

Nell laughed, the imagery pulling her back to the present moment from the tantalizing and traumatic past that had started to redraw itself in the form of mental pictures and intrude forcefully into her thoughts. Even so, she didn't know how on earth she was going to concentrate on what Joel had to say when her mind would be churning. For a few seconds she contemplated giving the lecture a miss, but then knew that she would be putting off the inevitable, when she really wanted to see Joel Matheson more than anything in the world.

'I'm glad you're with me, Trixie,' she said.

'Come on, then. I would give my eye-teeth for a mysterious past, to maybe compensate for the paucity of the present where mystery is concerned—or romance, for that matter,' Trixie said dryly.

'I'm not sure you would want my "mysterious" past,' Nell said, gathering up her papers, stating what she was thinking.

'Tell me about it some time. I'm all ears,' Trixie said.

They walked down a long corridor to find the appropriate lecture hall, then settled themselves in seats near the front, among about two hundred other people, Nell assessed. It was doubtful, she thought, that Joel would recognize her immediately after so long. Certainly, it was doubtful that he could pick her out in such a crowd from where he would be standing on the stage. After all, she was ten years older, looked more sophisticated and considerably different from the way she had looked at age sixteen-pretending-to-be-nineteen when they had met ten years ago. And what would he say when he saw her again? The thought nagged at her persistently as she contemplated what she would say to him.

Nonetheless, she felt an absurd desire to hide, to slide down in her seat, while at the same time longing to see him.

While they waited for Joel to be introduced, Nell's thoughts flitted back persistently to the past. She had always been ambitious, working hard at school for what she had wanted. Yet the experience of motherhood had mellowed her, making her focus on her child rather than on herself. Nevertheless, she had got through medical school, through her internship and was now two years into a residency training in the treatment of burns, and plastic surgery as it related to burns, with two more years to go.

Her mother had called it the water-lily syndrome, her ambition, while still being proud of her daughter. It was something she had made up. It meant that the person who had that syndrome was always wanting to pick the flower that was out of reach, rather than those she had in her garden, however beautiful. In her personal life, Joel had been that flower, always, it seemed…and proved…just out of reach. It was something she hoped she had outgrown, that striving.

Now the reaction of her body proved the lie as she waited for him to appear. Almost sick with anticipation, tempered by a strange apprehension, she tried to distract herself by concentrating on what Trixie was saying to her.

Then there he was, coming onto the stage a pace or two behind the man who was to introduce him. Oh, Joel, Joel! The words spoke themselves in her brain as she was torn between a desire to slide down in her chair and to stand up and shout, Joel, I'm here!

Without needing to be told, in spite of changes brought by the passage of time, she knew that the man who stood there was Joel.

He looked different in the harsh light above the stage, older, his face thin, the cheeks hollow. His boyish hair had been cut short. Yet that dynamic masculinity that had always seemed to emanate from him like a tangible thing was still there, that devastating attractiveness that was like a magnet to most women who came within his orbit. The well-cut grey suit he wore, that looked as though it had been made for him, with the medium blue shirt and subdued tie, enhanced that attractiveness. In the past he had seemed impervious to many of those women, but not to her…

As Nell stared at him she registered that he looked very tired and rather haggard. Next, she wanted to reach forward to touch him, to stroke his face, then to move into his arms, to feel them close tightly around her as they had done when they had both been younger.

'Is that him?' Trixie asked quietly.

'Yes.' Nell silently commended her colleague for not voicing the curiosity she must be feeling, for showing tact, which was not always her strong suit. 'In case you're wondering, he was once my boyfriend. I was never married.'

'I figured that. I was wondering,' Trixie whispered back, grinning, 'but I would never have asked.'

There was applause, signifying that she had not heard a word of the introduction.

Then he began to speak…with that decisive, deep, calm voice that she remembered. She bit her lip to stop it trembling and blinked rapidly to dispel the moisture that was gathering in her eyes, beyond her control. There was a gentleness in his tone, as always, signifying the empathy that he had displayed to his patients and to anyone he had liked, including her, when she had known him.

If Trixie sensed her emotion, she wisely said nothing. At first Nell let the meaning of what he was saying wash over her, then she began deliberately to concentrate. He had always been an excellent and patient teacher. Now, in spite of her agitation, she began to take in what he was saying, very soon finding herself absorbed by it.

When the lecture was over, some people in the audience crowded forward to the stage to talk to Joel, while the majority slowly began to file out of the room.

'Stay to talk to him,' Trixie urged Nell. 'I sense that you need to. I'll see you later. I think we're in a workshop together.'

'OK, Trixie. Save me a spot,' she said, forcing a lightness to her tone as she stood up.

Nell mounted the few steps to the stage, then hung back at the edge of the small group, waiting patiently until she was the only one left. It was amazing how quickly your sophistication could drop from you, she thought, that you could be transported back into the past, as she was when he looked at her.

His dark hair, which had been longish when she had known him before, giving him a rakish air, was not so now. Because of it, he seemed altogether more serious. As he looked at her, the years seemed to fall away, leaving her as breathless and vulnerable as she had been then.

'Hello, Nell,' he said quietly, extending a hand to her. 'It's been a long time.'

She took the two paces to get close to him and take his hand. 'Hello, Joel,' she said, her voice sounding rusty, as though she had not used it for hours. 'Yes, it has been a long time. I...I've been to a lot of conferences and I've never seen you.'

'I tend to go to conferences in the States and Europe, not to many in Canada,' he said.

'I see,' she said, not really seeing at all, her hand remaining in his, suddenly aware that the room still had a lot of people in it and they were under spotlights. Perhaps he had avoided conferences in Canada to avoid her. She eased her hand away, sensing that he had forgotten that he was holding it, as his eyes moved over her face, as though he wanted to imprint her features on his memory. She was aware, too, that she was being stiff and formal, against her nature, when she wanted to ask him a million questions and to put her arms around his neck. This was hardly the place.

His eyes were grey and direct, under very dark, definite brows, contrasting with the marked paleness of his skin, while his mouth was generous, firm, without being effeminate in any way. Those things had not changed, of course.

As a girl, she had noted approvingly that he had a strong chin and square jaw, had thought there was something of the poet about him. Now, in her maturity, she admired him anew.

Yet she was also struck again by how thin he looked. Was he ill? A new kind of fear, a dread, gripped her and overrode everything else. 'How are you, Joel?' she asked, her voice husky with emotion.

There was a slight hesitation. 'I'm well,' he said, with what seemed to her an odd inflection in his voice. 'How are you?'

Nell nodded. 'All right,' she said.

'You're very beautiful, Nell Montague,' he said, 'in a different way. I always knew you would be.' The smile he gave her transformed his face momentarily, erasing the tiredness, so that she felt the increased power of his attraction.

'Thank you,' she said.

'Hello again,' he said.

'Hello,' she whispered back.

'You're a doctor, too,' he said, 'specializing in burns. You followed through.'

'Yes. I'm still a resident, of course. I really love it, most of the time.' Somehow he had kept tabs on her, obviously. That was not too difficult in the professional world, although she certainly had not had any success in tracing him.

'Congratulations.'

'Thank you. It's been a long, hard slog, as you know.'

He smiled. 'It always is,' he said. 'Anything worth doing. Are you glad you did it?'

'Yes.' Thus, with casualness, they minimized the reality of their training, the blood, sweat and tears, the hours of stress and tension, the things they had both witnessed and tackled, the lack of sleep, the bone-weary sheer slog of it. For those who had been through it, it was a bond between them.

Nell recalled now the words of the head of department in the burns unit, Dr John Lane, to her when she had requested shorter hours to be with her son more when she had been training: 'You can't train part time, Nell,' he had said to her. 'You either do it, or you don't. The less you do, the more someone else has to do.' Nonetheless, he had made things easier for her whenever he had been able to, had given her days off, weekends off. And that had been even before he had let her know that he wanted to marry her…

And with polite phrases now, she and Joel minimized the impact of their meeting to the glaring eyes of the world, while her emotions churned, although there was a wealth of meaning in those words for both of them.

'Did you have anything in particular to say to me?' he enquired softly, with gross understatement, raising his eyebrows in the familiar way, not taking his eyes from her face. 'I feel you might.' There was a slight, partly cynical smile on his face.

Nell swallowed the proverbial painful lump in her throat. 'I…I'm not usually this tongue-tied. It's just that I wasn't expecting to see you, so it's taken me by surprise. I rather think we…we do have a lot to say to each other.'

He hadn't really changed. His gentle humour belied the changes in his appearance, from the handsome, insouciant youth who had looked like a poet to the hard, thin, pale man who stood before her. Especially, those eyes were the same, those grey, sensual, perceptive, intelligent eyes that were now regarding her with an unreadable expression. Most importantly, she had the impression that he was not displeased to see her.

Joel glanced towards the auditorium. 'If there were not so many people here, I would kiss you,' he said. 'Which is something uppermost in my mind at the moment.'

Nell laughed, relaxing somewhat. Mine too, she wanted to say, but the words stuck in her throat.

'No...no hard feelings, then?' she managed to get out, her cheeks flushing as they had done when she had been sixteen, impressed by the twenty-four-year-old Dr Joel Matheson, intern in the emergency department of Gresham General Hospital.

'Oh, I wouldn't say that, exactly,' he said, looking at her astutely so that her flush deepened. 'You treated me pretty badly, Nell Montague. I hoped you'd be here, I was looking forward to seeing you.'

Nell hoped fervently that none of her colleagues were down in the auditorium, watching her, as she felt that emotionally she had regressed to her early youth in the space of a few minutes, as susceptible to him as she had always been, and she felt that it would be obvious to the casual observer. A quick glance told her that the place had more or less emptied out.

'Will you have coffee with me?' he asked. 'My duty here is over. Or maybe a glass of beer in a pub?'

Nell moistened her dry lips. 'I'd like to,' she said, quickly making up her mind that she would have to miss the next workshop. No doubt Trixie would put two and two together and come up with five. 'Let's make it the beer.'

'Are you married?' he asked abruptly.

'No,' she said. 'And you?'

'No…I'm not married,' he said.

They had always been very closely attuned emotionally to each other, understanding intuitively how the other had felt, even in the relatively short time that they had known each other. They had been good at hearing the unspoken words.

Now she again picked up that odd inflection in his voice which, inexplicably, gave her an odd sense of listening to that soundless communication, as she had felt when she had seen his haggard face.

Mixed in with the joy of seeing him again was a niggling sense of apprehension. Also, in the space of just over an hour, her world had been turned upside down.

CHAPTER TWO

JOEL MATHESON watched Nell as she walked in front of him out of the large lecture hall, more nonplussed by the sight of her than he would ever have expected, unsure of how to proceed from here.

He had, of course, hoped and half assumed that she would be at this conference. Now the reality of her unsettled him and he felt his carefully maintained composure slipping as his eyes focussed on her soft-looking hair. Although he had tried to prepare himself for this, the reality of her—her beauty, her sweet vulnerability and sincerity, his memories—seemed to be stripping away his carefully constructed defences more rapidly than he knew how to cope with.

Perhaps he had been foolish to come here, to meet her again, when there could be no future for them together. That much had not changed. Yet he had not been able to resist when he had been approached by the organizers of the conference to be a replacement lecturer. In the past he had made a point of avoiding such gatherings in Gresham, had usually come to visit his parents and a few close friends and gone away again, hearing professional news of Nell very indirectly.

At the door to the street she turned to him. 'I feel a little guilty, skiving off like this in the middle of the week.' She smiled up at him. 'Some of my colleagues will be looking for me in the workshops. But I'm going to do it.' She laughed, her eyes dancing in the way he remembered. 'We can walk through the park and I know a little place on the other side where we can get a beer.'

'Great,' he said, feeling the urge to sweep her into his arms and kiss her.

'How long are you in Gresham?' she asked as they walked side by side away from the conference centre—like two children playing truant from school, he thought.

'For a week, this time,' he said. 'My parents are still here. Actually, I've been offered a job here in Gresham, in the burns unit where you work.'

'You have?' she said, stopping in her tracks to look at him in amazement. 'How come I haven't heard of it? John usually tells me, and the other guys in our department, what's going on.'

The way she said the name 'John' sent Joel's mental antennae strumming, and he had a vision of the grey-haired man who was the head of department, a widower, whom he sensed would be very attractive to women. With that sense came the stirrings of something that he had not fully felt for a long time…jealousy. What, he wondered, did the head of department mean to Nell in a personal sense? After ten years he had no right to feel jealous, but there it was.

They resumed walking. 'I was approached by Dr Lane,' Joel explained, 'as were several other doctors from various parts of the country. I came to take a look at the job out of curiosity, mainly.' Indeed, he had had no intention of taking the job. It was good once in a while to look at other places, otherwise one became stale and out of touch.

'I hadn't made up my mind until very recently,' he found himself saying smoothly. Like two minutes ago, he thought with a smile to himself, enjoying her wide-eyed surprise.

'You mean…you're going to take it?' she asked.

'Yes,' he said, enjoying her shock. While he was here in Gresham he would let John Lane know that he would be taking the job. 'I asked John not to say anything until I had had a chance to think about it.'

'How come none of us saw you here looking at the job?' she asked incredulously.

'I wanted it that way. I came after hours,' he said. 'I didn't particularly want my current hospital to know at the time that I was looking at another job.'

Then later, several months ago, he had warned his current hospital in Montreal that he was looking at the Gresham job, so that his notice to leave would be retroactive.

'And when would you be starting?' Nell asked. Joel sensed the deep emotion in her, while trying to gauge how pleased she was to see him. That emotion moved him, so that he felt the urge more than ever to take her in his arms, especially as she looked somehow fragile, the roundness of her earlier youth having given way to a womanly slimness.

'A month or so from now,' he found himself saying calmly, as though an alter ego had taken over and was speaking for him, had made up his mind for him. If he didn't take the holiday time that was owing to him he could start in a month, a prospect that was becoming more attractive by the minute...until he reminded himself yet again that there could be no future for himself and Nell, the realization bringing with it the familiar bitterness that he had tried so hard to let go, that he had worked on by living in the present, by concentrating on his job which he, fortunately, loved. Perhaps he was crazy to contemplate it, let alone do it.

The bitterness came when he looked at Nell, who epitomized the lie that work was enough. Being in Gresham, seeing her more or less every day could, he suspected, increase the agony of fruitless desires.

'That's…incredible,' she said. 'I had no idea.'

They entered a small park that they had to traverse in order to get to the pub she had in mind.

'Where will you live?' she asked. How odd it was that they were having this polite conversation, when really she wanted to go into his arms, wanted to rant and rave at him about why he had not contacted her for a very long time. He seemed to care, that was the odd part. It was difficult to ask pointed questions of someone you had not seen for a long time, when you didn't know what other attachments they had. She did not suppose that he lived in a personal vacuum.

'I own an apartment here,' he said casually. 'I'll live there until I can find a house I like, with a garden.'

'Oh…' she said. All the time that she had been searching for him he had had an apartment in Gresham and had obviously spent time there. Niggling feelings of anger tempered her happiness at seeing him, especially fuelled by the casualness of his tone.

'Are you engaged to be married?' he asked abruptly, torturing himself with a desire for knowledge that he was most likely better off without. 'Or have you a man friend? I hesitate to say "boyfriend", since you must be twenty-six.'

'Yes, I'm twenty-six,' she said. 'And, no, I don't have a specific man friend.'

Joel picked up something in her tone, which made him think again of John Lane—he was not sure why, except he suspected that the head of department would not let a prize like Nell Montague pass him by if he could help it. Although he was much too old for her, of course. Many a powerful man did not let age stand in his way, he well knew that, using his power as a lever to compete with younger men.

'In that case,' he said, taking her hand and pulling her under the shade of an enormous maple tree which had branches sweeping close to the ground, 'I shall give in to temptation.'

With that, he took her into his arms and kissed her, something he had fantasized about for a very long time, in the many lonely hours he had spent. At first she responded to him like a startled fawn, then she put her arms up around his neck and kissed him back with a fervour to match his own, so that he felt all his angst melting away, and a powerful sense of having come home. For a few precious moments he felt normal, relaxed, full of hope.

His thoughts went back to the time when he had first seen her, working in the emergency department of Gresham General Hospital, where she had been a volunteer worker for the summer and he had been a harassed intern, with all the weight of his twenty-four years seeming to bear down very heavily on his shoulders. Nell Montague had looked very fresh and sweet, very genuine, beautiful, tempered by common sense and a capacity for hard work, intelligent in a non-arrogant way that he had found wholly refreshing.

For Nell, standing in the circle of his arms, there was a familiar feeling of dissonance, when something she had wanted so much was actually happening. Her hands crept up into his hair, her fingers twining through it, as they had done years ago. With all her heart and soul she responded to him. This was how it had been for them before. It was all so fresh in her mind, as though there had not been a gap of ten years, had not been a lonely longing.

'Could you give me a hand?' Joel had said to her all those years ago that seemed like yesterday, coming up to her in one of the wide corridors near the reception desk and triage station of the emergency department of Gresham General Hospital. 'This man's waited long enough. I want to get him into a treatment room.'

She hadn't known his name then, of course, had only seen him vaguely from a distance, where his presence had not really registered on her as she had gone about her tasks. He had grasped one end of a stretcher on which a young man whose face had been pale and drawn with pain had lain, indicating to Nell that she should take the other end of the stretcher. At the time she had registered that the young doctor had looked harassed and serious.

Dumbly, she nodded, automatically going into action. 'I'm just a volunteer,' she said apologetically, moments later, to the young doctor who looked pale with fatigue, almost as pale as their patient on the stretcher. 'Just doing a summer job.'

'I know,' he said. 'That doesn't matter. I need help.' The look he gave her said everything that he did not want to verbalize in front of their patient—the shortage of staff, the lack of money that had caused the running-down of the department.

And I'm only sixteen, she felt prompted to add, but didn't do so. With her light brown hair piled up on top of her head in a neat chignon, instead of the ponytail that she usually wore at school, she knew that she looked older. Discreet make-up added to the illusion.

They introduced themselves, then later he asked her more questions about herself.

'What sort of training have you had?' he asked her. 'I assume you get one?'

'Oh, yes, we do.' She nodded, a little unnerved by him because she found him very attractive and wasn't sure how to handle that attraction. Compared with some of the other interns, who seemed to have two left feet sometimes, as well as two left hands, Dr Joel Matheson seemed mature and sophisticated beyond his years.

'You planning to be a doctor or nurse?' he asked. 'Or are you already in med school?'

'I…um…hope to be a doctor,' she said hesitantly, truthfully, yet not wanting him to know her age, sensing his personal interest in her and predicting his sudden loss of interest if she told him she was a schoolgirl.

'Are you in pre-meds?' he asked.

'I—' she began.

'I'm going to throw up,' their patient said, struggling up to support himself on one elbow, so that she didn't at that point have to answer the question. For the time being, Joel could speculate that she was already at university in a pre-med BA or BSc course.

That time with Joel was when she first developed an interest in the treatment of burns, including plastic surgery for burns, as that patient they wheeled on a stretcher into a treatment room had some severe, though localized, burns.

'How old are you?' Joel asked her later when they were momentarily alone.

'I'm nineteen,' she replied, surprised and shocked at herself at how easily the lie tripped off her tongue, as though she had been rehearsing it for a long time, knowing that her face was impassive and managing to prevent herself from blushing. Or it was as though she had been split into two personalities and the other one was speaking for her.

Now in Joel's arms, under the maple tree, her mind and emotions in turmoil, feeling as though she were in a dream, she marvelled again at the lie she had told so glibly. Guiltily she pulled back from him, feeling again the familiar regret of a past that could not be undone. On his face was an unguarded expression of admiration and desire, before he looked away, his arms dropping from her.

'Which way from here?' he said, as they moved on to resume their walk.

'This way,' she said, pointing, striving for composure. There was a tension between them now that one could have cut with the proverbial knife.

As they walked in the bright sunlight, her thoughts persistently went back to the past, as the sense of unreality was so strong here in the present, especially when Joel's hand brushed against hers and he said 'May I?'

before taking her hand in his. Her compliance was her answer.

'I know this is crazy,' he said, 'but I can't resist.'

Nell refrained from asking him why he thought it was crazy, frightened of the answer. There was in her a barely controllable desire to weep. How on earth was she to tell him about Alec? Her tempestuous state of mind was in conflict with her joy in the clear blue sky, in the green grass, brilliant in the sunlight.

More than anything, she had wanted Joel to remain interested in her, had wanted to see that light of unconscious admiration in his eyes as he had looked at her. Her all-girls school had not prepared her for that. Yet with Joel Matheson she really had felt that they were kindred spirits, destined to mean something to one another. All that intuitive knowledge had come from having worked together for a few hours of intense interaction. In her youthful enthusiasm, she had blurted out all that to him. Solemnly he had agreed that they were, indeed, kindred spirits. If he had been amused by her intensity then, he had not given any indication of it.

Unlike some of the self-centred, brash and uncouth youths she knew, brothers of her school friends, Joel Matheson had seemed to be in a league of his own.

'You must be in university, then?' he asked.

'Um…first year,' she said, with remarkable sang-froid. 'BSc. Hoping to get into medical school.'

Again she sensed instinctively that he was interested in her as a woman, an intelligent person, as well as a colleague of sorts. She also sensed that he wouldn't go in for cradle-snatching, and a three-year period made all the difference in one's maturity at her stage of life, which she knew from her sister, Lottie, who really was nineteen, very grown-up and serious about life in general and her studies in particular.

Now, walking with Joel, herself a responsible senior resident surgeon-in-training—with only two more years to do before taking her final fellowship exams—with the burns team at a respected teaching hospital, she felt seriously chastened by the memory of those lies that had tripped so thoughtlessly and uncharacteristically from her tongue.

'What have you been doing all these years?' she asked Joel now as they walked. 'I…I tried to find you, but no one knew where you were—or if they did, they were not going to tell me.' Some of the hurt and bitterness that she had felt by that fruitless search came through now in her tone, and she didn't care.

'From Gresham I went to Montreal to do some further training in burns treatment, as you knew at the time,' he said. 'Then I went to various places in the States, before coming back to Montreal more recently.'

'Ah,' she said. 'So you're not going to tell me why you didn't want me to find you?'

'Not at this moment,' he said.

'Some time, perhaps?' she persisted.

'Perhaps,' he said.

A closeness engendered by the embrace was slipping away, while the emotional tension increased, so it seemed to Nell.

At the pub they bought two glasses of beer and carried them out to a small patio in a back garden, the only people there, and seated themselves at a small bistro table under a tree, with the scent of lilac around them.

'This is great. I'm glad you brought me here,' Joel said, fixing her with that appraising stare from his astute grey eyes that had so devastated her in the past and was doing a lot now to undermine her defences. And she was going to need those defences, she told herself wryly.

'It's a small oasis in the middle of this city,' she said, returning his regard. In the brilliant, unforgiving sunlight, she confirmed that he looked strained, as though he had in the past been ill. Until he told her about it, she could not bring herself to ask personal questions about his health.

'Do you remember when we worked together that first time,' Joel said, 'when a nurse called you from helping me, to get two urinals for patients who were stuck on stretchers in the corridor?'

As he must have intended, Nell thought, the memory disarmed her and she laughed. 'Oh, yes. I'm not likely to forget that. I was never so humiliated in my life. Especially as I was trying so hard to impress you.'

Joel smiled. 'Yes…' he said. 'I know.'

So he knew that much.

'Nell!' One of the registered nurses had bawled at her just as she had been about to help Joel with another case. 'Would you take a couple of urinals to those two guys on the stretchers at the end of the hall, left side? As quick as you can.'

'Sure,' she had called back, making eye contact with Joel as she had backed away from him, responding to his rueful grin with one of her own. She had known he had been amused by her, by her earnestness, but had not laughed at her.

'So much for getting above myself,' she had added. 'That puts me firmly in my place.'

'See you in treatment room two, if you can come back to help me, Nell,' he had said, grinning broadly. 'You're very much appreciated.'

With a slightly false smile, she had walked away, with her face more than ordinarily hot.

Now, sitting with the mature Joel Matheson, soothed by the scent of lilac and the beer, she relaxed and laughed. 'Saved by the urinal!' she said. 'Saved, maybe, from making a fool of myself, assuming knowledge I did not have. At the time, I wanted to giggle hysterically as I marched briskly to the nearest utility room. You must have thought me an uppity little thing!'

'No, not particularly,' he said. He filled the ensuing silence by taking a swallow of beer. That's when I fell in love with you, but didn't really know it then, he wanted to say. 'More likely, I thought you a sweet little thing. You looked so vulnerable and wounded at that moment that I wanted to give that nurse hell.'

Nell laughed again, remembering how embarrassed she had felt. She also remembered asking herself why she had told two lies like that about herself. It had come home to her fast that once you had told one such lie, you had to tell other lies in order to maintain that first one. What she had told him about herself had, in fact, been her sister Lottie's story.

It turned out that those lies, part of an interwoven matrix of deceit, had been the harbingers of all that had happened after…

CHAPTER THREE

'WILL you have dinner with me tonight?' Joel asked, as they left the pub to walk back through the park. 'If it isn't too short notice.'

'Um...yes...I'd like to,' Nell replied.

'You don't sound too sure,' he said, smiling at her as they entered the park and began to walk briskly towards the far side.

'Oh, I am sure,' she said. 'I'd really like to.' For the umpteenth time, she mulled over the question of how she was going to tell him about Alec. The enormity of the problem engendered a sense of panic. The moment had to be just right...

'You'll have to choose the restaurant,' he said. 'I'm somewhat out of touch with the food scene in Gresham. I could pick you up, if you like,' he said. 'About half past seven?'

'No! Um...no...it's all right,' she said quickly. 'I'd rather meet you at the restaurant. I…know a good place. I'll just write down the address for you and we'll meet there.'

'Fine,' he said, looking at her sideways, noting her flushed cheeks. Steering her over to a park bench, he sat down. 'I'll give you the address of my apartment, and the phone number. Perhaps I could have your address.'

'Yes,' she said, feeling the panic rising in her, not finding a reason to deny him her address. He wasn't likely to turn up there unannounced, she told herself. At some point, he and Alec would have to meet, but not before she had paved the way very carefully. Up to now, it had all been hypothetical. Now the reality of the task was beginning to take on the semblance of something nearly insurmountable, because there had been no time for her to prepare.

On pieces of paper torn from a notebook, they exchanged addresses.

'Here's the name of a restaurant I know pretty well,' she said, writing on another piece of paper, handing it to him. It would be necessary to call her mother to ask if she could stay with Alec while she herself went out to dinner. Or he could stay at her parents' place for the night, as he often did. She seldom went out in the evenings during the week, preferring to spend the time with her son.

'Could we make it six-thirty, if that's not too early for you?' she asked. That would give her time to make supper for Alec and relieve her mother from babysitting at a reasonable hour. 'Since it's a weekday. I'll be starving by then. I'll make a reservation.'

'That's fine,' he said.

As Joel took the piece of paper, their hands touched.

'Nell, Nell…' He murmured her name, and in a moment they were in each other's arms, oblivious to the few passers-by in the park. On the uncomfortable park bench he held her tightly against him and kissed her.

Nell pulled away and put her head on his shoulder, trembling. Too much was happening in too short a time. 'I can't take all this in,' she said falteringly. 'I tried to find you…then I gave up and assumed that I would probably never see you again. There were…things I wanted to tell you. Now you tell me that you're coming to work at Gresham General.'

Joel stroked her hair. 'It's all right,' he said. 'We'll talk this evening.'

'Yes,' she whispered. 'Now I've got to get back to that symposium. John might ask me what I've learned, and I want to be in a position to give some intelligent answers.'

'Right,' he said.

Back at the conference centre they parted, Nell having a winded feeling as she walked away from Joel, going through the motions as though in a dream. Some people were breaking for lunch now, while she was booked into a second workshop that was to extend over the first lunch period. As it was, in her present state she couldn't possibly eat anything.

'Hey, where have you been, stranger?' Trixie accosted Nell as she entered the workshop room. 'I trust you made contact with the long-lost one.'

'I did,' Nell said as they both searched for the table where their names would be displayed.

'That accounts for the punch-drunk look,' Trixie commented.

'You may have to cover up for me, Trixie,' Nell said. 'I'm going to have a serious concentration problem.'

'Will do,' Trixie said, looking at her curiously. 'That will make up for the times you've covered up for me in the operating room when I hardly knew a scalpel from the dissecting forceps.'

The day seemed to go by with great speed, during which Nell took a lot of notes, forcing herself to concentrate, so that later she would have a record of what she had heard and participated in, instead of thinking that most of it had gone in one ear and out the other.

When the conference was over at four o'clock she drove to her parents' house, close to her own, to pick up Alec, who went there after school. They lived in an old, established residential neighbourhood near the centre of the city, very convenient for downtown and the teaching hospitals. For the umpteenth time Nell acknowledged her good fortune in having such loving parents who had stood by her in all her vicissitudes. Without them, she could not be training for a very demanding profession, doing post-grad work as she was now, as they had always helped her raise her son.

They had also been able and willing to educate her well, together with her two sisters, to help her now to pay for a house by lending her the down-payment. One day she would be in a position to pay them back.

'Mum!' Alec was in the front garden of her parents' big old red-brick house as she pulled into the circular gravel driveway and he ran towards her as she got out. 'Guess what?'

Nell opened her arms to her nine-year-old son and then hugged him as he ran into them, a poignant sense of love, mingled with undefinable emotions, swamping her. 'I couldn't possibly guess,' she said, smiling. 'Especially since my brain's scrambled from a day of lectures.'

'My English teacher told me today that I'm going to get the English prize for the year,' Alec said, his grey eyes alight with something like wonder. 'It was what I was hoping for. He said he liked my poems and all my other work. I'm supposed to keep it secret for now. Will you be coming to the prize-giving, Mum?'

'When have I ever missed it?' She smiled down at him. 'Congratulations. I'm very, very proud of you. I have something to tell you as well, but not yet. I'll tell you on the weekend.'

'Something nice?' Alec squinted up at her.

How like his father he looked, Nell thought again, with his dark hair and eyebrows a contrast against the pale skin of his face. Anyone who saw them together would know. So far, no one ever had. There seemed little of her in Alec, except sometimes in his expressions and gestures.

'I think you'll find it nice,' she said, relieved that she could put it off for a few days until she had thought things through, decided how she was going to go about it.

'Granny's coming over to our place later on when you go out,' Alec said, 'because I want to do my homework over there.'

'That's great,' Nell said. 'Get in the car, then I'll just see Granny for a few minutes.'

'Hello, dear,' her mother said, giving her a kiss on the cheek. 'I'll come over just before you want to leave.'

'Thanks, Mum.' Her mother was an older version of herself, her grey hair streaked with a becoming honey blonde, with fair skin and blue eyes. She had been a nurse, still worked occasionally. She had been a second mother to Alec, while Nell's father, a GP, had played the father role to Alec as best he could. 'I'll give him supper and make sure he starts on his homework.'

In the car for the short drive to their own house, Alec seemed to pick up some vibes from her as he looked at her with more than the usual perspicacity. 'Who are you going out to dinner with?' he asked.

'A...um...former colleague, whom I haven't seen for a long time.' She replied evenly, keeping her eyes on the road. 'We met unexpectedly at the conference I attended today, the one I told you about.'

'Oh,' he said.

In the house, a smaller version of her parents' old mellow red-brick home, they were greeted ecstatically by their two Dalmatians, Runty and Cherry, who were mother and daughter respectively.

'Hello, darlings,' Nell greeted them, patting each one in turn. 'You must be desperate to get out.'

Having let the dogs out to the back garden, Nell rushed around in the kitchen preparing supper for Alec, while he sat in their family room off the kitchen making a start on his homework. There was a rule that he could not watch television or do anything else until he had finished the homework.

While he was eating his supper, Nell had a quick shower and changed into a light-weight cotton skirt and blouse, then started to blow-dry her hair, keeping a close eye on the time. As soon as her mother came, she would leave for the restaurant.

'Mum, there's someone at the door,' Alec bawled up the stairs, while their two dogs barked furiously.

'Can you see who it is, please?' she called back. 'I'm not quite ready.'

Above the sound of the hairdryer she could hear voices in the front hall, Alec telling the dogs to be quiet, then Alec clomping up the stairs.

'Mum, it's a man,' Alec said, standing in the doorway of the bathroom. 'He said he's the one you're going out to dinner with and he's lost the piece of paper you gave him with the name of the restaurant on it so he came round here.'

Nell stared at her son, her face blank with shock, almost dropping the hairdryer. Alec looked tousled and vulnerable standing there, still dressed in his somewhat crumpled school uniform of grey trousers, white shirt with the sleeves rolled up and a loosely knotted striped tie. The black Oxfords that he wore were dusty.

Carefully she switched off the hairdryer, feeling a strange urge to sweep her son into her arms and squeeze him very, very tightly. 'Thank you,' she said. 'Show him into the sitting room, would you? And tell him that I'll be down in a few minutes, please.'

'Do I know him?' Alec asked quietly, frowning. 'He looks like someone I've seen before, but I can't remember.'

'You've never met him,' Nell said.

When he had gone, Nell stared at herself in the mirror, seeing her large, frightened eyes staring back at her, her face a new shade of pale. Everything had come together with such frightening speed that she didn't know how she was to cope. And she had thought that afternoon that Joel was not likely to turn up unannounced at her home. Famous last words.

There was no way out of this—she had to walk down the stairs and give some sort of explanation to Joel.

'How are you getting on with the homework?' she said to Alec a few minutes later, having come quietly down the stairs and into the family room.

'OK,' he said. 'I've got a proposal to write up for a science project. Granny said she would help me with that.'

'Good,' Nell said, feeling a poignant regret that she would not be the one to help him. She didn't do his homework for him, just helped him to get it organized. 'I…I'll just go and speak to my guest while we wait for Granny.' Her mother would let herself in with her own key.

Alec gave her a strange look, but said nothing. One could not fool children, she thought. Alec sensed that the stranger in the sitting room was someone other than an ordinary colleague whom she had not seen for a long time. There were photographs of the young Joel in the house, yet now he looked sufficiently different that it might take her son some time to make the connection. She did not doubt that he would eventually make it.

Guiltily, she left him, wishing that she could just blurt out the truth to him in a rush but knowing that she had better go carefully. Her desire to protect her son from any sort of hurt was uppermost in her mind.

Joel was standing at the large bay window of the sitting room, his hands in his trouser pockets, staring out at the front garden that was mellow in the early evening sun, where everything was very lush and green. As she shut the door carefully, he turned slowly to look at her. A few moments of silence ticked by, emotional and fraught.

'You have a child?' he asked carefully, at last.

'Yes,' she said, standing by the door, holding herself tensely. 'I...thought I would tell you later on this evening, but you seem to have pre-empted me.'

'Yes, I'm sorry to have turned up unexpectedly like this,' he said. 'I mislaid the piece of paper with the name of the restaurant on it.'

'Perhaps it's just as well,' Nell said resignedly, feeling slightly sick with nerves.

'Why didn't you tell me earlier?' he asked quietly. 'You said you'd never been married.'

'I haven't,' she said. 'Telling you…when I hadn't expected to see you before today…was not easy, so I put it off.'

Just then there was the sound of the front door being unlocked, her mother having walked over, and the delighted barking once again of the Dalmatians. Saved from further explanation, Nell opened the sitting-room door.

'Come out to meet my mother,' Nell said, relieved beyond measure.

As her mother greeted the dogs in the hallway, Nell managed to gain a measure of composure. 'Mum,' she said, 'this is Dr

Matheson. We have to rush because we have a reservation.' The name, that should have meant something also to her mother, was mumbled, half-lost in the barking of the dogs.

'How do you do?' her mother said, shaking Joel's hand, while Nell held her breath. So far, the name meant nothing to her mother. Maybe after they had left the house it would trigger a memory.

'Pleased to meet you,' Joel said, while Nell opened the front door, having written the name of the restaurant in a notebook where her mother could call, if necessary.

'I've got my pager, Mum,' she said as they went out. 'Thanks a million.'

Out in the warm evening sunlight, Joel took her arm to slow her down. 'Shall we take my car?' he said, his voice tight. 'No point in taking two. You can direct me.' He steered her over to his car.

'All right,' she said, with her heart pounding, knowing that this was the moment of truth, the time she had thought about over the years, had tried to plan for. Now she felt her mind to be blank with regard to strategy, disarmed and vulnerable. Here she was, with no strategy whatsoever.

Joel's face was without expression as he started the car and drove it quickly out of her driveway. Over on the next street, a wide, leafy residential street with no obvious traffic, he eased the car to the side of the road and stopped. In the ensuing silence, he turned to look at her, his expression stony. 'That boy must be about nine or ten years old,' he said. 'Would that be right?'

Nell nodded, unable to utter a word. Joel continued to look at her as though he were stripping her naked and looking through to her soul as well.

'Is he my son?'

Again she nodded, looking down at her clasped hands in her lap, now aware that she had been wringing her hands, as some of the angst of the past came back to her. It was odd how the past never really died, how it reverberated down the years, sometimes down the generations. 'Yes.' The word came out in a whisper.

Letting out a pent-up breath, Joel leaned back in the seat, putting his head back against the head-rest, a hand over his closed eyes. The silence was more unnerving to Nell than if he had ranted and raved. 'Let me get this straight,' he said at last, without looking at her. 'You must have known you were pregnant when you told me your parents didn't want you to associate with me any more. When you told me you were only sixteen. Before I actually left for Montreal.'

'Yes, Joel, I'm afraid so,' she confessed quietly. 'And I'm sorry. As I said before, I tried to find you after Alec was born, to tell you, because I thought you had a right to know.'

'You let me go away without telling me,' he said incredulously. 'I'm finding that very hard to understand. Why, for God's sake?'

'For one thing I...didn't want you to feel obligated to me in any way,' she said, feeling the urge again to weep, wishing he would look at her, put his arms around her as he had done that morning on the park bench. 'My parents advised me…ordered me, more like it…not to tell you. My father was very angry. I wouldn't tell them who you were. I didn't want them to accuse you in any way. It was only when Alec was three that I told them…because I wanted to tell Alec, to show him photographs of you…' Nell's voice trailed to a halt. How inadequate it seemed, explaining all that now, when ten years had gone by in which Joel could have known that he had a son, Alec could have had a father.

As though it had happened only recently, she recalled again her father's words to her. 'You give him up,' he had said, in a voice that had allowed no alternative.

'Of course, once Alec was born, my parents loved him, were absolutely delighted with him,' she went on quietly, while Joel still sat with his eyes closed, his face shuttered. 'They've been so good to both of us.'

At last Joel opened his eyes and turned to her, his expression uncomprehending, hard. 'I don't mind having a child,' he said slowly, harshly. 'In the circumstances, I like it. But I find it quite incomprehensible that you didn't tell me. We were supposed to love each other, and all that.'

'What circumstances?' she said.

Joel did not answer. Instead he looked at his wristwatch and then started the car. 'We're late for the restaurant,' he said brusquely. 'We'll talk after we've eaten.'

At first Nell thought that she could not eat anything as they sat in the small, intimate restaurant where she had been many times before with friends. She was glad that she could not see anyone she knew. When she ordered food she realized that she was almost faint with hunger, not having had a proper lunch, so she managed to eat everything that was put in front of her, hardly noticing what it was.

They said little during the meal, forgoing wine. A musician was playing a violin, absolving both of them from having to talk.

'Shall we walk for a while, maybe down by the waterfront?' Joel suggested evenly as they left the restaurant.

'I'd like that,' she said, very aware of the tension in him. Inside she was agonizing over their relationship which had seemed so promising that morning, while outwardly calm. The tension of trying to remain calm was telling on her and she was glad that she did not have to concentrate on driving.

They drove a short distance to a large sand spit that went out into Lake Ontario, just south of downtown Gresham, a place that was a bird sanctuary, intersected with footpaths and bordered by a narrow stony beach. Joel found a place to park and they walked silently along the beach, where there were no other people in sight, where wading birds ran up and down near the water. The tranquillity of it, with the traffic noise of the city only a faint hum in the distance, calmed her.

'Shall we sit?' Joel said, indicating two smooth low rocks that would make good seats.

It was pleasant sitting there, looking out over the water in the mellow evening sunlight, with a breeze blowing away vestiges of city pollution that penetrated the area. Breathing deeply, Nell willed herself to calm down.

Joel stared out over the blue-grey water of the lake, hardly able to comprehend that he actually had a son, when he had more or less resigned himself to the thought that he would never have children. When he considered that for ten years he had not known of the child's existence, he felt a slow, bitter anger, During those years they could have got to know each other, the boy would have grown up knowing that he had a father who cared for him.

'I would have taken responsibility, you know,' he said evenly, trying to keep the harshness and bitterness out of his tone, reminding himself that Nell had been only sixteen, that he had made love to her…with her consent…had supposedly been responsible at the time for the contraception. Although she had been beyond the age of consent, he would not have touched her if he had known her true age. The thought of it made him feel guilty and angry with himself, as well as with her.

'Did you think I wouldn't?' he persisted.

'After all this time, I can't say exactly what I thought. All I remember is that I think I knew you would take responsibility, but I didn't want you to have to take responsibility,' she said, sitting immobile beside him. 'I didn't want you to feel obligated or trapped.'

'We would have sorted something out,' he said tightly. 'We could have shared everything. I imagine that you could have used some emotional and practical support from me.'

'Yes,' she agreed. 'It may seem odd now...but it seemed to me then that I had to keep it a secret from you, partly for reasons that I've just given and partly because my parents had told me to give you up. And the reality of what it would mean to my life hadn't really set in, of course.'

'Shall we walk a bit?' he said, standing up and reaching out a hand to her.

'Mmm,' she said. Although his expression was stiff and controlled, he kept hold of her hand as they walked, and the warm contact added poignancy to his words that they could have shared things, and she wanted to weep because of the lost opportunities.

They walked along a thin strip of sand near the water's edge, where the water of the lake lapped softly. Soothed by nature and the touch of Joel's hand, she strove to explain herself.

'It's such a relief to talk about it,' she said. 'My parents didn't want any man in my life at that point, because that was not what they had planned for me. They said I was far too young, and I was, Joel. I was so naïve. I had a lot of confidence, but I was so naïve.'

'That doesn't make any difference,' he said. 'I could still have been a help to you, and I think I had a right to know.'

'It's easy to see that now,' she said quietly, 'but at the time I was very, very frightened.

I just did what my parents thought best. It was difficult being at school, looking pregnant. Fortunately, he was born in the middle of the summer…the fourteenth of August.'

They walked in silence for a while, watching the sun turn red, low in the sky.

'After the baby was born, I wanted to tell you…face to face, not in a letter,' she explained, desperately wanting him to understand. 'Perhaps I should have sent a letter to your parents' home, but I didn't want to. When you sent me that card telling me you didn't want to maintain contact, it broke my heart.'

'Let's go back,' he said. They turned round to walk back to where they had parked his car.

'There's something I want you to know,' she said. 'Alec was always wanted.' She recalled the joy she had felt in her condition in quiet moments when she had been alone, an intense, strange, primeval joy.

'Very glad to hear it,' he said.

'I loved him even before he was born. In fact, I'm so glad that I have him. Now I can't imagine what my life felt like before I had him. It seems like I had another self before,' she explained quietly, searching for words among those that seemed so inadequate.

Joel thought of the time she had told him that her parents had forbidden her to see him again, that she was only sixteen. 'Why did you lie to me?' He remembered saying that to her when they had met one weekend in his apartment, a bitterly cold winter day in which she had been bundled up in a thick, loose sweater, leggings and a voluminous sheepskin coat. Perhaps she had worn all that, he thought now, because her figure had been changing even then. 'I can't believe you're a kid, still in high school.'

'I just had my seventeenth birthday,' she had said.

'Gee, that makes a big difference,' he had said, the first time he had used sarcasm to her, a way to hide his bitterness. 'And I asked you why you lied to me.'

'I wanted to get to know you outside work,' she had said. 'I couldn't bear the thought that you wouldn't be interested in me.'

Now they got back into his car for the drive back to her house, remained sitting there for a few minutes, reluctant to leave that quiet and pleasant place and the tentative communication that had, at last, opened up between them in that place. Nell knew that such communication should have started a long time ago.

'The outcome of this is that I find I can't trust you, Nell,' Joel said as they sat side by side, the sadness of his words like a tangible thing between them. 'You've lied to me once too often, this time a lie of omission, and it's just burning me up.'

'Will you still be coming to work here?' she asked, her voice small.

Joel sighed. 'Yes,' he said. 'One thing you can do for me from now on is let me be part of my son's life.'

'Yes,' she said. 'He knows your name, has seen photographs of you. Maybe when I get home he will have recognized you, because he asked me if he knew you.'

'That's a start. We'll play it by ear,' he said. 'There's no hurry. Maybe I can see him later on this week before I leave Gresham?'

'Yes,' she said softly.

'Will you tell him that I'm his father, or would you like me to do it?' he asked, staring out of the windshield at the mellow evening sunlight.

'I rather think he will have realized by then,' she said. 'Otherwise, I'll tell him.'

'All right,' he said.

'What about…us?' she asked quietly.

'Do you want there to be an "us"?' he said brusquely.

'I…I think I do,' she said.

Again he sighed. 'I don't know, Nell,' he said. 'I really don't know. At this moment, I doubt that there can be any "us".'

CHAPTER FOUR

JOEL drove Nell back to the house and declined to come in, switching off the car engine and the lights so that they sat in silence.

'You'll have to forgive me,' she said desperately, 'otherwise it will be impossible for us to work together. Anything that we might have done differently in the past might not have worked out. Alec's been well cared for.'

'I'm sorry, too,' Joel said quietly, 'that you had all that to go through by yourself. I know you had your parents. This is a strange situation and I'm having trouble getting my head around it.'

'Not so strange,' Nell said. 'People have babies all the time in different situations. It's only strange when it happens to you, unplanned.'

'I'm sorry,' Joel said again. 'But seeing your son now, I wouldn't wish that he hadn't been born.'

'I'm not sorry,' she said.

'I should have been more careful,' he said, 'as well as guessing that you were much younger than you said you were. Maybe I didn't want to know.'

'Don't blame yourself,' she said, her voice trembling. 'That's the last thing I want. There is no blame… It's just something that happened.'

Responding to the unbearable tension between them, Nell moved to get out of the car, giving Joel a quick kiss on the cheek. 'Goodnight,' she said. 'Don't think too badly of me. I'm so relieved now that you know. It's been hanging over me all these years like a sword waiting to fall.'

'Wait,' Joel said, leaning over and pulling her into his arms, crushing his mouth on hers with a fierce kiss. Nell put her arms up around his neck, holding him to her.

'It's good to see you again, Nell,' Joel said when he had released her. 'We can try to be friends, yes? For the sake of the boy. I'm glad I have a son, although it's going to take some getting used to.'

'Yes…we'll try to be friends.' As Nell got out of the car, putting on a calm face, she felt as though she was weeping inside, because what she wanted from Joel was more than friendship. But that would have to do for a start, if indeed they could achieve that. At the moment she wasn't too sure. Before going in, she watched him drive away.

Her mother was waiting in the hallway when she got in, as were the two dogs, who only gave a cursory bark or two before going back to their beds in the kitchen. 'Hello, dear,' her mother said, giving her a kiss on the cheek. 'Alec's asleep, having done all his homework.' Not one to beat about the bush, she added, 'Who was that man, Nell? Alec seems to think he's his father, he's been getting out photographs. Now I think so too.'

Nell sighed. 'Yes, Mum, it's him.' Briefly she told her mother about the unexpected meeting, about the fact that Joel was coming to work at her hospital.

'What a shock, eh? That could be a bit awkward for you,' her mother said, 'although maybe the best thing for Alec.'

'It could be awkward, but I think we can work through it. Joel wants to meet Alec, be a part of his life if it works out.'

'If you handle it right, I don't see why it shouldn't work out,' her mother said.

'The trouble is, he doesn't trust me,' Nell said miserably. 'He said so.'

'You'll have to show him that you can be trusted,' her mother said, preparing to leave. 'After all, you're ten years older, things are completely different now.'

'I know. Goodnight, Mum. And thanks… thank you for everything.'

Slowly she went into the kitchen and dumped her handbag on a counter, deciding that she would make a cup of tea before going to bed. Going through the familiar motions of filling the kettle, plugging it in, calmed her churning mind. What a strange day it had been, yet the relief that she had spoken of earlier was very real.

It was all over now, the need to inform Joel. Part of the battle was over. What she had left to do was talk to Alec about it. How astute he was. You couldn't really fool children: they picked up intuitively on all the unspoken cues and clues, the nuances of behaviour and speech in those close to them. She didn't want to fool him anyway. A long time ago she had vowed to be truthful with him about everything, it was better in the long run, because otherwise you were not trusted. It was an awful thing not to be trusted…

Tears gathered in her eyes and she blinked them away with determination as she reached into a cupboard for a mug. Automatically she went through the motions of making tea, mentally rehearsing what she would say to Alec.

'Mum.'

Nell turned round. There was Alec in the doorway, tousled in his pyjamas, having come upon her soundlessly.

'Oh, hello, darling,' she said. 'I'm just making myself some tea. Would you like something? How come you're awake?' She went over to him and kissed him, giving him a hug at the same time. Hesitantly, he came into the room, as though he wasn't sure of what he had to say to her.

'Was that man my father?' he said, looking at her solemnly, his eyes so like Joel's that her heart lurched with love for him.

'Come and sit at the table,' Nell said. 'Would you like juice?'

'No.'

'Wait until I have my tea,' she said, making up her mind. 'I'll tell you what happened.' Alec already knew the story of his birth, because she had told him. As far as he was able to understand, he had accepted that, but she sensed he did not accept that his father had not tried to get in touch with them, had not accepted that he did not have the love of a father, as most other boys did with whom he went to school.

Nell sat down next to him at the kitchen table, cradling the mug of tea in both hands. 'Yes, that man is your father...Joel

Matheson,' she said at last. 'We met unexpectedly at the conference I went to today,' she began. 'He's never been to such meetings before in Gresham.'

'He didn't say he was my dad,' Alec said, puzzled and very serious. Nell got the impression that he had not been asleep at all, had lain in bed worrying about this. 'Is that because he didn't know who I was?'

'Yes. But like you, he guessed after a while, because you look so alike. I didn't tell him about you at the conference—I thought I would leave it till later. I didn't know he was going to come to the house. I'm sorry he suddenly appeared like that, Alec.' She paused for a sip of tea. What an added relief it was to talk to Alec about this. 'You know that I tried to find him, but couldn't. Then he just turned up…'

Alec looked at her, his expression still serious as he studied her face, weighing up her words. 'Does he want to meet me? I mean, today didn't really count, did it?'

'No, it didn't,' she said. 'Yes, he very much wants to meet you. Maybe we can work something out this week, before he leaves for Montreal, where he lives right now.'

Carefully she explained to Alec that Joel would be coming to work in Gresham.

'I'm glad about that,' Alec said, sounding so intense that Nell leaned forward and kissed him.

'So am I,' she said. 'Maybe we'll all like each other.'

He looked puzzled again. 'It would be funny if we didn't,' he said.

'Well—' she chose her words carefully '—just because you want to like someone and they you, it doesn't always work out that way. It's like love. You can't force someone to love you, just because you want them to, or because you love them.'

There must have been something in her tone, because Alec looked at her enquiringly. 'Does…he love you, Mum?' he asked.

'He used to,' she said. 'Now I don't know. We have to get to know each other again.'

'What about me? Will he love me?'

'I hope so, but I don't know,' she said.

They sat talking for a while as Nell drank her tea, until she felt content with what she had told Alec so far. 'We'll just do our best to make sure it works out,' she said at last, standing up, 'so that we all like each other. We'll see how it goes from there. Come on, it's time you went back to bed. I'll come up and sit with you until you're asleep.'

'OK,' he said, going ahead of her. It was a measure of his disturbance that he did not decline her offer, saying that he was too old to have her sit by the bed until he fell asleep. It was something she had done for years when he had been younger.

There was a low stool by the bed and she sat on it, taking his hand. 'Off you go to sleep,' she said, 'otherwise you'll feel really tired tomorrow at school. It's all going to work out.' She stroked his hair away from his forehead and kissed him. Already she had a strange intimation of what it would be like to share her child with his father, and that sense brought mixed feelings, although it was something she had longed for. The focus of his love would not be all on her and her own parents.

'I'm glad he's here at last,' Alec mumbled.

'So am I,' she said. What ever the future might bring, that much was true.

With his hand warmly in hers, she leant back against the wall and mulled over all that had happened that day, what she had said to Joel, what he had said to her, both spoken and unspoken. Whatever happened next, it was all out in the open, and it seemed to her that there was nowhere to go but forward.

When Alec was asleep and she was in bed herself, she knew that she would not sleep well because her mind was too active and for once she did not worry about it. There was so much to think about, to sort out. Tomorrow she would call Joel and make plans for the three of them to go out on Saturday, knowing that he planned to return to Montreal on Sunday evening. As luck would have it, she was to be off for the weekend. Maybe they would do something simple, like take the dogs for a long walk, and then she would cook supper for all of them.

The weekend dawned bright and pleasantly hot. Gardens were burgeoning with life, as were the wild places in the city of Gresham, now that it was summer, everything green and lush. The collective spirit went into overdrive, Nell could feel it, as the population of the city finally put memories of the long, cold winter behind them.

Joel had duly been invited to come for the afternoon and had accepted.

Where Nell lived, in an old established residential area near the downtown section, the city was liberally intersected with wooded ravines with pathways and lanes through them. The one that she went to frequently with her family and dogs had a stream running through it, which looked inviting, even though it was actually polluted with the overflow from city drains that took rain water. It looked good as it babbled over stones. While walking there, she could delude herself that she was in the country, especially in the summcr when dragonflies flitted about over wild flowers and birds sang. Once she had seen a fox nonchalantly crossing the lane a few yards ahead of her.

'He's here, Mum!' Alec shouted excitedly to her after lunch on Saturday. They had both been waiting somewhat impatiently for Joel to arrive, with Nell getting more and more agitated, as well as stressed with the effort of not wanting to show it to her son.

She acknowledged that she was just as excited as Alec was at the prospect of spending time with Joel, who had agreed readily to the outing. Nell got the sense that there was to be some sort of truce between them, if she could call it that. For a few hours they would be a family, linked by their blood ties. It was almost a new concept to her, something that had come to seem like a vain hope before, that she would be forever united with Joel because of their child, regardless of what happened to them as individuals. Sometimes that concept was comforting.

Nell hurried from the kitchen into the sitting room where Alec was looking out of the large bay window onto the driveway of the house where Joel's dark red Buick was just coming to a halt.

'Go out to meet him, Alec,' Nell said, even as her son was already rushing to the front door. 'I think it's better if you meet him by yourself. Don't let the dogs out.'

The two dogs set up a cacophony of barking, the old dog, Runty, who was now fourteen years old but still active, and the younger one, Cherry, who was seven years old.

At the front door Alec stopped in his headlong dash. 'Mum,' he said, 'I'm scared. What if he doesn't like me?'

'That's a risk you have to take,' she said, grinning at him, giving his shoulder a squeeze. 'What if you don't like him?'

'I expect I will like him,' he said.

'I expect he'll like you,' she said reassuringly. 'Go on. Remember that he'll be just as nervous as you are, if not more.'

'Will he?' Alec said, incredulous.

'Yes, because you've known all your life that he was your father, but he didn't even know that he had a son. So remember that before you judge him, Alec. He didn't know because I didn't tell him.'

'All right,' Alec said, sounding very grown-up, as though he fully understood that the success of the venture was up to him fifty-fifty with his father.

Nell opened the door for Alec to go out. 'Maybe you'd like to stay out there in the garden for a while,' she suggested gently. 'Show Joel your organic vegetable garden and the flowers you're growing. I know he's interested in those things.'

She watched him walk in a determined fashion towards his father who was just getting out of his car, then she shut the door, feeling instinctively that this was something they had to do without her.

Joel saw the boy coming towards him, squinting against the bright sun, his steps slowing a little as he came. It seemed utterly amazing to him that this boy was his son, and he felt an odd mixture of gratitude to Nell that she had produced this child, who was so like him that it was uncanny, and a sense that she had betrayed his trust, young and naïve though she had been. As he watched the boy approach he knew that maybe he was being unfair to Nell, but he could not argue with the way he felt. Trust was something that one earned.

'Hello, Alec,' he called, walking forward. 'I'm very pleased to meet you at last.' He held out his hand as they met. 'Your mother will have told you that I'm…your father.'

Alec took his hand hesitantly. 'Yes,' he said, letting go of Joel's hand after a moment. 'Mum said I'm to show you the vegetable garden.' His voice was stoic, as though he was going to see this through, no matter what, as he looked at Joel curiously.

'That's a great idea,' Joel said, grinning, touched by the boy's earnestness. 'I would be very interested in that. I have a garden myself in Montreal, which I'm going to be very sorry to leave when I move here to Gresham.'

'You can start a new one,' Alec commented.

'Yes, I can, and most likely will. Maybe that's something you could help me with,' Joel said.

'Yes,' Alec said. 'It's this way.'

They walked round the side of the house to the back, where there was a large garden, part in shade, part in sun, with the vegetable garden at the bottom and a small greenhouse. Joel reminded himself not to overdo the bonhomie, which would grate on the sensibilities of the child. He had witnessed it time and time again in other adults and it had certainly grated on him as an observer.

'Do you have any dogs?' Alec asked as they came to a halt beside a small vegetable patch that was obviously Alec's garden.

'No, but I do have a cat named Felix,' Joel said, 'who has great character. He's all black. He won't come in at night unless I whistle "Good King Wenceslas".'

Alec looked startled, and then burst out laughing. 'Is that true?' he said.

'Absolutely,' Joel said. 'It's caused me a certain amount of mild embarrassment, I can tell you, especially in the middle of summer. A few people who live around me think I'm off my rocker, but a few others know I've got a neurotic cat.'

'I wish I could meet him,' Alec said wistfully. 'I've always wanted a cat, but it's difficult with the dogs. Granny has a cat.'

'Oh, you will get to meet him,' Joel promised, warming to the unspoiled personality of his son, silently commending Nell and her family on the good job they had done with him. 'I'll be bringing him to Gresham when I come to live here.'

'That's good,' Alec said.

'Show me what you're growing here,' Joel said, squatting down to get closer to the vegetable patch. 'Let me see if I can identify some of these plants, then you can correct me if I get it wrong.'

'All right,' Alec said. By his tone, it seemed that he was rclaxing.

Nell went out to the driveway, standing in the sunshine, to watch father and son coming towards her. By their body language, it appeared that they were reasonably at ease with each other, and some of the sharp anxiety in her died down. Life would go on if they didn't like each other, but she hoped for better things.

Alec was chattering, looking up happily at his father. Casually dressed in light linen trousers and a linen shirt in a stone colour, Joel looked to her devastatingly attractive. Sometimes over the last ten years she had often thought that she would never find a man really attractive again, even Joel, so now the feeling came as relief, proving to her that she was not dead inside after all.

'Hello, Nell.' Joel put out a hand to her and leaned forward to kiss her on the cheek, while she wondered somewhat cynically if he was doing that to impress Alec, or whether he really wanted to kiss her. Then she told herself sternly to just calm down and enjoy the day, the moment.

'Hello, Joel,' she said.

When he smiled, her heart seemed to turn over, and she grinned back. 'Come in,' she invitcd. 'Get acquainted with the dogs again.'

'They sound as though they want to tear me apart.' He laughed as Nell opened the door and let the Dalmatians out to frolic around Joel, obviously identifying him as someone they had met before.

'Would you like a drink of something, Joel…tea, or whatever? Or shall we just start our walk now?'

'Let's walk,' he said. 'I can't wait to get down to that ravine again now that the sun's shining.'

'Can you get the dogs' leads, Alec, please?' she asked.

While her son was away, leaving them alone for a few moments, Joel looked at her as a man would look at an attractive woman. 'He's a great kid,' he said softly.

Nell nodded, saying nothing.

'Thank you for inviting me here, I'm going to enjoy this.' His glance encompassed her front garden, the warm red brick façade of her old house.

'So am I,' she said, looking him full in the face. 'I'm very glad you came.' Like him, she was casually dressed in cotton twill trousers and a simple cotton blouse with the sleeves rolled up, yet she had taken care with her appearance.

They put leads on the dogs and set out for the ravine walk, which started about two hundred metres from the house, with a rustic lane going down from the side of a street, through mature trees and bushes, to another lane that ran between high banks of land that were thick with trees.

Once there, they let the dogs loose, who, overjoyed to be free, raced around in circles for a while and then Alec threw a Frisbee for them to catch, and sometimes he threw it to Joel. They were all laughing, while the dogs were almost delirious with delight at having so much concentrated attention.

Then Alec took off into the distance, running with the dogs, well ahead of Nell and Joel.

'I have to congratulate you, Nell,' Joel said. 'You've done a very good job with him.'

'Thank you,' she said, gratified. 'But I couldn't have done it without my parents. Also, Alec has a very calm, sweet personality, very sensible.'

'Like you?' he said, turning to her, smiling slightly.

'I thought more like you,' she said.

'Don't put yourself down,' he said.

'Just being honest,' she said, then smiled ruefully, looking at him to see if he had made the connection between that comment and the lies she had told in the past.

He had. 'About time, Nell Montague,' he said.

'It hasn't been easy,' she said, hearing the defensiveness creeping into her own voice. 'There were many, many times when I was in despair about how I was going to cope. Worst of all was the guilt I felt when I was working and studying, thinking I should be with Alec more. I don't know how I got through it, really. As it was, I spent every spare moment with him.'

'I can imagine,' he said. The unspoken words were between them that things might have been somewhat easier for her if she had told him.

'It's easy in retrospect to say what could have been,' she said, responding to the unspoken, 'but at the time I had no idea what it would have been like if you had known. At least I didn't have to work in the summers when I was a student. My parents subsidized me so that I could be with Alec.'

Their son was running back and forth, huffing and puffing, the dogs chasing him, then he came up to Nell and Joel and walked between them, holding a hand of each, chattering about the turtle he had seen once in the ravine by the stream, even though it was polluted, and the fox that he had seen. His presence there between them, so full of life and promise, strengthened for Nell the strange and powerful bond that she had always felt between herself and Joel. Glancing sideways at him, she tried to discern whether he felt the same.

There were no clues for her in his expression, apart from what she thought was contentment as he looked down at Alec, caught up in his enthusiasm.

Before Alec ran off again he took Joel's hand and Nell's hand and put them together. 'I want you two to like each other,' he said, walking backwards, looking up at them quizzically.

As he ran away from them, they walked self-consciously holding hands. The warmth of Joel's hand against hers made Nell feel womanly, soft and vulnerable. At that moment she wanted to cry.

Joel's grip was firm and he pulled her closer to him. 'He's also very bright,' he commented huskily, laughter in his voice.

Not trusting her voice, Nell merely smiled and nodded in agreement, liking the feel of his arm brushing against hers. The ten years that they had been apart, in spite of the more recent time that they had spent together, seemed to hang between them like a tangible thing, a barrier, as well it might. This older, harder Joel was more unfathomable.

'You've changed a lot, Joel,' she said after a while, as they sauntered in the sunlight.

'So have you. We grow up eventually.'

Sometimes, left alone, certain things worked out, she considered. In some ways she had dreaded this outing, yet now it was more or less relaxed and rather wonderful. Bright sunlight warmed them as they walked. The green leaves of summer shivered in a soft breeze.

* * *

They were all pleasantly tired when they got back to the house.

'I'll make some tea,' Nell offered, going through to the kitchen at the back of the house. 'Then I'll start preparing the supper. We'll have our tea on the patio.'

In the rear garden next to the house, extending the full width of the building, with walk-outs from the kitchen-family room and the sitting room, was a flagstoned patio with potted plants and chairs placed here and there on it. The sun was shining onto it, making it a welcoming place.

'Can I watch television for a little bit, Mum?' Alec asked, helping himself to a large glass of orange juice from the fridge. 'There's a short programme I have to watch for a project at school. It's about conservation of the rain forests in British Columbia.' He looked at Joel. 'Would you like to watch with me?'

'I'd like to help your mother first,' Joel said, smiling at him, not unmoved, she could see, by the appeal. 'I may watch with you for a short while.'

'Can I, Mum?'

'All right, but please fill the dogs' water bowl first,' shc said, glad that Alec was behaving naturally in this situation.

'OK.'

Once Alec was out of the room, Joel helped Nell collect items for tea. 'I'm not a bad cook…if you remember, Nell,' he said.

'I do remember,' she said, very aware of his nearness. The spacious kitchen did not seem big enough for the two of them. 'You could make a salad, if you like. I'm going to grill some salmon. Let's have our tea first, shall we?'

On the patio in the warm sun, looking down over the garden that had so recently been under a thick layer of snow, life seemed good to Nell and she felt a little as though she were living in a dream, had felt that way somewhat from the time she had seen Joel's name on the conference programme. The dogs followed them out, to lie in the sun, tongues lolling.

'How are your parents?' she asked, not knowing quite what to say to Joel.

'They're becoming quite frail,' he said. 'Which is one reason why I decided to come back to Gresham, particularly as my brother travels a lot with his job, so can't spend much time with them.'

Nell poured them tea from a tray she had brought out, using the activity as a cover-up for the seriousness of her question. 'It appeared to me that you didn't want me to find you, Joel,' she said. 'May I ask why? Was it because it was all over between us and you wanted it to remain that way?' She dreaded the answer, yet was confused by his obvious delight in seeing her at the conference, the passion of his embraces, his kisses.

'That's something I would prefer to discuss at some other time,' he said. 'Just at this time I want to get to know you again…and Alec. Can you wait?'

'I guess I'll have to,' she said, puzzled.

Frustrated and ill at ease, Nell knew that for now she would have to be contented with that answer.

CHAPTER FIVE

NELL stood in one of the wide corridors in the burns unit at Gresham General with a group of ten first-year medical students.

They did not go into the rooms where the patients were in isolation in the burns intensive care unit; they looked through the wide windows that opened onto the interior corridor.

'We can't go in here,' Nell said to the group as they peered into a room, 'because one of the serious problems with burns is...what?'

'Infection,' one of the students piped up.

'Yes, that's right,' Nell said. 'Infection is a major cause of death, too. Also, thermal burns to the skin are frequently complicated by...what?'

'By smoke injury to the lungs,' another student said.

'Yes,' Nell affirmed, moving on slowly down the corridor with her small group. Teaching was part of her role at the hospital, even though she was still a resident-in-training. 'Now, let me see if you've been doing your reading. How soon after thermal injury does host immunity become depressed?'

Nell shepherded her group down the corridor and out of the burns intensive care unit to join the burns rounds. Some interesting case histories were going to be presented by one or two of the residents-in-training at these rounds, where as many of the members of the department as possible would attend.

They all walked quickly to a small lecture theatre not far from the burns unit, where rounds for teaching purposes were generally held, usually starting at half past eight in the morning, or earlier.

'For those of you who didn't manage to get breakfast,' Nell said, smiling at her group, 'there will be food at the back of the lecture room…coffee and tea, fruit juice, pastries and fruit. After rounds we'll go to the wards to visit some of the patients who are not in Intensive Care. We'll meet up with Dr Matheson and Dr Deerborne.' How odd it seemed to her, saying Joel's name.

With the students settled, Nell made a bee-line for a coffee urn, desperate for a cup of coffee.

It had been two weeks since Joel Matheson had started work back at Gresham General. His arrival had caused quite a stir among the staff, as any good, new person was like the proverbial broom that was reputed to sweep clean. As for herself, she was mired in the routine of work, putting in long hours, being on call, dealing with emergencies, some of them horrendous, with not much time left over during working hours to dwell too much on her personal relationship with Joel. So far, they were working well together.

Burns cases were brought in from other parts of the province, many arriving by helicopter, landing on the roof of the hospital where there was a helipad.

So far, she had seen Joel a few times outside work since he had moved back to Gresham. They had gone out as a threesome with Alec, almost like a family, she had thought at the time, except that there were undercurrents between herself and Joel, inevitably. They made her realise how much they had both changed. Alec, on the other hand, seemed delighted to have a father, was the only one of the trio who seemed able to act naturally all the time.

Where it would all end, she had no idea. Speculating about it was a constant strain, bringing with it weariness. For most of the time when she was not at work her thoughts were centred on Joel, Alec and the relationships between the three of them. Sometimes it was a relief to be at work where she could, from long practice, tune out almost anything other than the job in hand.

Joel had taken Alec one day to meet his parents, without her, telling her that he would take her to see them at a later date. It would be enough for them to contend with, he said, to find out that they had a grandson. In the past, when she had been sixteen, she had met them once.

Nell had been particularly sensitive to the impact of Joel's presence on the female staff in the plastic surgery and burns unit, on both the medical staff and the nursing staff. There were not many unattached, attractive young doctors available, even in a hospital as large as Gresham General. Thus, she had found herself in an odd position, confirming to herself that she did indeed not have any claim on him, in spite of the powerful link that having a child with him provided.

As she sat down in the front row of chairs in the lecture theatre, nursing her cup of coffee while she waited for rounds to begin, Nell recalled again the popular clichés of 'going with the flow', 'playing it by ear', that were bandied about. They provided the framework of how she was planning to proceed, as far as one could plan.

She let out an involuntary sigh. Now she was very glad that few of her colleagues knew she had a son, as they might discern the link between him and Joel. One who did know about him was the head of department, John Lane, whom she had told in confidence once when she had needed a few days off because Alec had been ill. She could imagine the surprise of her other colleagues if she told them about Alec and that Joel was his father. She had no intention of telling them. Only a few close friends knew about Alec, were part of his life.

The room filled up quickly, then there was a stir as Joel came in with two of the burns unit junior residents who were to present cases. With them was Trixie. To her chagrin, Nell felt a twinge of jealousy at the familiar and friendly way that Trixie was talking to Joel, and the attentive way that he bent his head down to hear what she had to say as they came and sat in the front row, not far from her. He was smiling, looking very attractive.

Nell took a swallow of coffee and looked away. Already she felt exhausted and the day had hardly started. Part of that was because she had worked over the weekend. Part was due to nervous tension.

'Hello, Nell. How are you?' Nell looked up to find Joel standing in front of her.

'Oh…' She struggled for words. 'Hello, Joel. Nice to see you. I had a hectic weekend.' She pushed her untidy hair behind her ears, aware that she wasn't looking her best. Usually she didn't think too much about her appearance once she was at work. Now she was uncharacteristically self-conscious, especially as his eyes were going over her face. 'It didn't help to have a teaching session at eight o'clock this morning with some first-year medical students.'

'I expect they hung on your every word,' he said, grinning, something that made his familiar grey eyes light up, and she felt a lifting of her mood. Annoyed at her involuntary response to his charm, she looked down at the cup of coffee in her hand.

'I think they did,' she said, unable to resist smiling back. 'They were pretty attentive, anyway. Everything's great, really. I'm just being a grouch. How are you, Joel?'

Joel settled himself in the chair beside her. He always had an intense aura, it seemed to her, of masculinity about him that attracted her to him like a flower to the sun, and she felt it now that he was only inches away from her. Never macho, he seemed to have an unconscious, easy acceptance of his manliness, which had the effect on her of making her feel intensely womanly.

'I'm well,' he said. Again, there seemed to be a certain nuance in his tone that puzzled her and she told herself that she was imagining it.

'It's surprisingly good to be back in this hospital, challenging but good,' he went on. 'I wasn't sure how it was going to be. So far, I have no regrets about making the move from Montreal.'

'I'm glad,' she said stiltedly. 'It was quite a coup for John Lane to get you to come here. You're a good doctor.'

'You have quite a reputation here as a good doctor too, a good surgeon, so I'm finding out,' Joel said, looking at her so intently that she felt almost shy under his scrutiny. 'Quite a change from the girl who had to run to get the urinals in the emergency department.'

'Maybe,' she said, her face warm, unable to repress a smile at the memory, in spite of a mild embarrassment about her youthful confidence that she sometimes thought of now as over-confidence. 'Don't remind me of that. What carefree days they were. As for the career, it's been a long haul,' she said. 'I've a lot to learn yet, being pretty junior still, but I'm enjoying it. We have a really great team here.'

'So I'm finding out,' he said.

'Sometimes, when things get tough, I wish I was back giving out urinals,' she volunteered honestly, with a sigh. 'We see such horrible things sometimes.'

'Yes,' he murmured gently. 'All part of the job.' Then he put a hand over hers briefly and squeezed it.

Damn him! She wished he wouldn't look at her so astutely, or touch her, especially when they were surrounded by other people, although she doubted that anyone had noticed the brief intimate gesture that was, after all, quite common among commiserating colleagues. At least, she wished he would not touch her until she had had a better chance to make up her mind about him. Seeing him outside work had sensitized her to his presence at work.

At the moment she was happy that her son should have a relationship with him, but where that left her she wasn't at all sure, after he had stated that there probably wasn't going to be any 'us'. What she did know was that the sight of him smiling attentively at Trixie left her feeling decidedly crabby.

'Any regrets about your choice of specialty?' he asked. 'You could have done psychiatry or maybe bacteriology, more or less nine-to-five jobs.'

'No regrets,' she said. And I don't have any regrets about meeting you, she confirmed again to herself. The clarity of it surprised her. Well, at least that's out of the way, she told herself.

Joel sighed, much as she had done a few moments before, as though he had a load on his mind, as she did. 'Well, here we are, Dr Montague,' he said quietly, so that no one else could hear. 'With you, I feel like an actor who finds himself back in an old play, having forgotten his lines, and the script as well.' Leaning back in his chair, he put his hands casually into the pockets of the white lab coat that he wore over a green scrub suit, and stretched out his legs, looking the epitome of relaxed sophistication.

Looking at him, she had an intimation that he was just as churned up inside as she was, and the knowledge warmed her towards him, bringing with it a sense of being less alone. At last, perhaps, he would share some of the responsibilities with her of being a parent to Alec. Sometimes, when she allowed herself to think about it, she dreaded the future of having to deal with a teenage boy as a single mother.

'Yes,' she agreed, not looking at him. 'That's a good way of putting it.'

'Why did you decide not to tell many people here about Alec?'

'It's none of their business, for one thing,' she said shortly, deciding not to tell him at that moment about John Lane. 'And for another, I was concerned that they might think I wasn't capable of doing certain things, putting in the required hours. That would probably have been the case if my parents hadn't been so wonderful about it all. They saved me, and him, so to speak. And I have a part-time housekeeper. I believe that babies and young children need to be with people who love them, and my parents dote on him.'

Another doctor, Rex Talbot, a general surgeon on the burns team, took the vacant chair on the other side of Joel. 'Morning.' He nodded at both of them.

'Hi, Rex.' She smiled back at him. He was a member of the team whom she liked very much, and who had recently been away on holiday. He was very married, with a slew of young children. 'You've met Joel Matheson?'

'Yep, we've met,' he said.

'Are you still on for the excision and debridement this afternoon?' Joel asked her, referring to a case of his that she had agreed to help with in the burns operating suite, a case of third-degree burns that required extensive excision of necrotic tissue. She had agreed the day before, having asked a colleague to take over an outpatient clinic of hers so that she could free herself to help. This was often the case in the burns unit, they helped each other as emergency cases came in. Rex would also be there in the operating room.

'Yes, I've managed to free up some time,' she said.

'Great. I appreciate it,' he said.

She thought he would get up and move back to sit next to Trixie before the talk started, but he stayed where he was. This was all going to be very, very strange, she decided. Over the past two weeks she had not seen a great deal of him at work, as he had been meeting many other colleagues, getting into the routine of working in a new place. Joel had spent a lot of time with John.

Without any more ado, for all had a busy day ahead, two of the burns unit residents began to present two cases, with slides and graphs, talking about the history of the patients, their treatment, infection rates, progress.

Soon Nell was absorbed in the cases, although still acutely aware of Joel next to her. You have no claim on him whatsoever, she reminded herself silently. Did she want one? The unwelcome twinges of jealousy seemed to answer her question. She had thought she had known herself pretty well, then something had happened and she had found out that she hadn't. She had thought herself above jealousy. She shied away from all the unspoken questions. Concentrate on the job, she told herself sternly.

When the presentation was over, she excused herself and went to the back of the room to meet up with her group of students, who were scheduled to be with her for the remainder of the day.

'In the burns operating room,' she said to them, 'you'll be in the observation room and we can talk to each other through the intercom. We don't want you in the actual operating room because of the risk of infection that you might bring in. So only essential staff will be inside.'

The students exchanged glances a little nervously.

'We're looking forward to it,' one said. 'We haven't been in the burns OR before.'

'I'll take you there now,' she said, 'to show you where you can change. You'll need to put on scrub suits, overshoes and hats,' she said. 'When I've done that, we can go to the floor again in the intensive care unit and you can read the case history of the patient we're going to operate on. He's a thirty-six-year-old man who has extensive third-degree burns from being in a house fire. Who can tell me what third-degree burns are?'

One of the students, a petite, earnest young woman who reminded Nell of herself at that age, spoke up. 'It's when the epidermis, the papillary and reticular dermis and different depths of subcutaneous tissue have been damaged,' she said.

'Right,' Nell said, nodding. 'Can injuries like this heal spontaneously, as we know some burns can?'

'No,' the young woman said, 'they won't heal spontaneously.'

'So how do we deal with that situation?'

'Treatment involves excision of all injured tissue,' the student said.

'Right. Good,' Nell said. 'So what we're going to do during the operation is remove that dead tissue, which is a source of infection, and we'll cover the underlying tissues with autografts, and with dermal substitutes as well, since he hasn't a lot of his own skin left.'

She went on to explain that autografts were skin grafts taken from the patient's own body, while homografts were donated skin from someone else. Then there were various types of commercially produced artificial skin which were all used to cover raw tissue when the burnt tissue had been excised. Pigskin was also sometimes used, she explained.

Although the medical students had no doubt done some reading on the subject, Nell always made it a policy to give a brief explanation of everything she was doing, so that they could then ask further questions if the information was new to them.

Joel came up to them and introduced himself to the students. 'It's my case,' he said, 'so you can also ask me any questions. It's a rather bloody operation while we're removing all that dead tissue, because when we've cut off the dead tissue, the healthy tissue underneath bleeds rather profusely. We stop that bleeding with dressings impregnated with an adrenaline solution, until we can get the grafts in position.'

They all nodded wisely, and then all moved off in a body to go to the operating unit which was part of the large burns unit, next to Intensive Care.

'I'm using the Watson dermatome,' Joel explained to the medical students, describing the specialized plastic surgery knife that he was using.

The students were safely ensconced behind the glass wall of the observation room that was located at one side of the operating room, where they could communicate through an intercom. 'And Dr Montague is using a Goulian knife, which you can see is smaller, and is very useful for the hands and face,' Joel continued. 'This dead tissue that we're removing is called the eschar and the operation is an escharotomy.'

Nell cast a quick glance at the medical students. They were all wide-eyed, with a somewhat stupefied expression of surprise, while a few of them looked decidedly greyer in the face. Carefully she returned her attention to what she was doing.

As the case neared completion several hours later, Nell allowed herself to relax a little. Concentration had been complete for a long time, so that they had scarcely been aware of time passing. For a moment she closed her eyes and flexed her tired shoulder muscles. Everything had gone well. They had grafted what they could with autografts, and had used various synthetic materials and dermal substitutes elsewhere. There was a great satisfaction in a job well done. Although the patient looked a mess now, in a few weeks he would look totally different.

'Thank you all for your expert help,' Joel said to her, Bill Currie—the senior burns resident—Rex Talbot, the scrub nurse and circulating nurse.

He looked at each of them in turn, and Nell felt a warmth and something like pride in him, as though she had a right to it. There were a lot of surgeons who did not thank anybody for a job well done, or for anything else. She could tell that Joel was going to be well respected and popular. The thought came to her then that her judgement as a sixteen-year-old girl had been instinctively right about Joel Matheson. She had gravitated to him then like a homing pigeon.

The door to their operating room opened and John Lane entered, tying on a fresh face mask over his nose and mouth.

'Hi, everyone,' he said. 'How's it going?' He smiled at them. He always liked to support his staff, to keep in touch, to find out what exactly was going on, and how.

'Pretty good,' Joel replied for all of them. 'We'll be finished here very shortly.'

'Hello, Nell,' John said, coming to stand near her. 'How are things with you?' There was a warmth and intimacy in his voice, to which Nell always responded, as she did now, being reminded of how much she liked and respected him. He always remained professional in the workplace, and she respected him for that, yet he was relaxed and friendly, without being familiar. There was much bantering in the operating rooms, which helped to counter the stress engendered by some of the horrendous injuries they had to deal with, the sights they had to witness.

'Oh, fine, just helping out,' she said airily, an answering warmth in her voice. 'It also gave me a chance to show the students something.'

'I think we scared the hell out of them,' Bill Currie broke in. 'They left some time ago. Maybe we'll have a few more recruits for psychiatry, dermatology and maybe bacteriology.'

John chuckled.

'They'll be back. After all, look at you.'

'Oh, well,' Bill said, 'I do it mainly to be close to Nell. And I like the way she handles a knife. It keeps me mesmerized.'

'That makes two of us,' John said, laughing. 'The closeness, I mean. Although I don't get to do it often enough these days now that she's more competent than I am.'

Nell laughed. 'Don't say that. I won't be able to live up to it.' She turned to smile at John, who, although close, was not close enough to contaminate her sterile gown.

As she turned her head back to face the operating table, her eyes met Joel's for a few seconds and she was surprised by the sharp look in his, a speculation, a questioning, and something else…cynicism. Annoyingly, she felt a wave of heat envelop her, flooding up to her face which, thankfully, was well covered by a mask, goggles and a paper mob cap pulled well down over her ears and part of her cheeks.

With that sense of annoyance was an odd feeling of shame, which took her by surprise, thinking that she, perhaps, was at least partially responsible for his cynicism. Once, it had seemed to her, he had been idealistic, believing the best of people. Don't assume it's you, she told herself. Ten years have gone by, with plenty happening to him to make him cynical. Yet she could not shake the feeling. At that moment she was aware only of

Joel, so intensely aware that she thought everyone else in the room must know of it. And she sensed that he felt the same about her.

Determined not to make eye contact with him again until after the operation, she turned with slow deliberation to take a wad of dressings that the scrub nurse was handing to her. They needed to pad the grafts well so that those thin layers of precious skin were properly protected.

Concentrating on placing those dressings, prior to bringing the operation to an end, she kept her head bent, forcing the movements of her hands to be deliberate, practised and efficient. What's it to you? she wanted to say to Joel angrily. What right have you to look at me in that judgmental way? It's nothing to do with you, she wanted to add, yet at the same time feeling that it was a lie. She and Joel had a son. Any man that she was involved with from now on would be of interest to Joel and to Alec. Up to now, Grandpa had also been Daddy to Alec. Now all of a sudden he had his real daddy in his life and everything had changed.

Concentrate on the job, for heaven's sake, she told herself. Pushing all thoughts of her personal life out of her head, she meticulously helped Joel and Bill to place the thick pads of dressing material over their patient's body.

When the operation was over, with the patient safely wheeled back into the burns intensive care unit to recover, Nell went into the area of the scrub sinks outside the operating room and took off her face mask and paper hat and threw them into a waste bin. Then she took off her protective goggles and put them into the pocket of her green scrub suit. Every muscle in her body, it seemed, was aching, as well as her feet. It would be good to get home.

With a sigh, she allowed herself to relax, running her fingers through her hair which had become plastered to her scalp with sweat. The case was Joel's, so she did not have to do any of the follow-up work. Bending over a sink, she splashed a little cold water onto her face and ran her hands under the water.

'You coming for a cup of tea or coffee, Nell?' John was there beside her, washing his hands. 'I might take a few minutes off myself.'

'Yes, I'm dying for a cup of tea,' she said, wiping her hands on a paper towel. 'Are you finished operating for the day?'

'Yes. Just have a few more floor visits to do to see how my patients are doing,' John said, as they moved out of the immediate unit to an outer corridor to go to the staff coffee-lounge. 'What do you think of our new doctor, if that's not an unfair question?'

'He's a very good surgeon,' she said carefully, 'and very good with patients.'

'Yes,' he said. 'All reports are good so far. He's certainly living up to his reputation.'

John, who was tall and slim, yet muscular and fit, walked with ease beside her, matching his stride to hers.

'I don't think I told you that I knew Joel Matheson a long time ago when he was an intern here and I was a volunteer in the emergency department,' she said, deciding to tell him now in case it came out later, when it would seem odd that she had not mentioned it. 'He was a good doctor then.'

Although she had told John about Alec in a superficial way, she had not divulged the name of his father or the circumstances of his birth. All he knew was that she had never been married. Perhaps John would put two and two together at some point and decide that Joel could be the father of her son. The past was coming back to haunt her.

As they entered the coffee-lounge together, before John could comment further, she remembered the trouble she had got into in her youth by telling lies. The fall-out of that was still with her, so now she tried to be more up-front where necessary, finding how to do it in the most tactful way. She wasn't 'seeing' John, although she strongly suspected he would like that arrangement, and she considered that she did not have to give him any more details of her private life than she had already. However, a very astute man, he would perhaps pick up the inevitable vibes between herself and Joel, be they positive or negative.

'Just made a fresh pot of tea, Dr Montague,' a nurse said to her.

'Ah, that's what I like to hear,' Nell said. 'Thanks.'

The coffee-lounge, which was for the medical and nursing staff of the burns intensive care and operating rooms, held a few people in varying states of relaxation, drinking coffee or tea, reading newspapers, eating snacks.

Nell got her own mug out of the cupboard and poured herself some tea. As she relaxed back in a chair, with her aching feet up on a footstool, she reflected yet again on the strange quirk of fate that had brought her and Joel within each other's orbits again.

Bill and Joel came into the room just as John sat down beside her, and she had the distinct impression that he was going to ask her something unrelated to work. Joel looked from one to the other, his eyes narrow, then his gaze locked with hers for a moment before he turned away to pour himself a cup of coffee.

'How's our patient doing?' she asked Joel.

'Pretty good,' he said. 'We're hoping he can breathe on his own now.' For a short while their patient had been on a ventilator. 'Thanks again for helping me, Nell. I appreciate it.'

'My pleasure,' she said, meaning it. 'I shan't hesitate to make a similar request when I need help.'

'Don't hesitate,' he said.

Joel looked pale and tired, engendering in Nell a stab of fear as she assessed him. Was he all right? A helplessness that she had never experienced before momentarily blotted out all other thoughts and feelings. I still love him, she thought with certainty, and I most likely always will.

There was chatter in the room as the staff relaxed a little before going back to work. No one was looking at her, Nell decided as she glanced around, trying to control a trembling of her lips. Perhaps working with Joel was going to be more emotionally fraught than she could cope with easily, she thought. Today she had spent more time with him in the workplace than she had over the past two weeks.

Carefully she drank her tea, glad of its calming effect. In a few minutes she had to go to see some paticnts, bcfore going home for the day. Those who were in isolation in the intensive care unit took a long time to see as she had to put on a protective gown, mask, latex gloves and hat, a different set in each room, in order not to transmit any sort of infection.

As she left the coffee-lounge, Joel followed her out and walked with her down the corridor to go out of the inner sanctum, as they called it, to the main burns area. At such moments he looked dear and familiar to her, Nell thought as she glanced at him. At other times he seemed like a stranger who seemed very preoccupied with his own deep concerns, too preoccupied to consider her or where she might be in his life, if anywhere other than as a colleague and mother of a child who was also his.

'Will your mother be looking after Alec at the moment?' he asked.

'Yes,' she said. 'Right now he's at a summer day camp, an art camp, and he gets picked up and brought back home by a special bus. During the school year he comes home on a school bus, to my parents' place, then I pick him up from there. He often has supper there. For some mornings I have a part-time housekeeper who arrives early and oversees Alec, getting him onto the school bus. It's a fine balance, a juggling act, keeping him supervised...but I'm not complaining.'

'Sounds like a good arrangement,' Joel commented.

Knowing that she was protesting too much, at pains to assure Joel that Alec had not been neglected, she nonetheless could not stop herself from explaining. 'Yes, it's a great arrangement, secure,' she said. 'Alec likes it and my parents like it, although I do sometimes worry about how we'll cope when he gets into his teens and doesn't necessarily want to do what he's told all the time.' She chuckled, trying to make light of something that was a worry to her. 'People I know with teenage sons and daughters are forever warning me.'

In a quiet side corridor, with no one about, Joel stopped and took her arm. 'Is there anything between you and John Lane?' he asked baldly.

'No, not really,' she prevaricated. 'He's a nice man with whom I sometimes go out for a drink or a meal.'

'And?' he said.

Nell flushed. 'There is no "and",' she said, annoyed that he could get beneath her guard so easily. 'We're not lovers, if that's what you think, although, to be honest, I think he would like us to be.'

'Would you?'

'No,' she said honestly. 'I don't think so. The difference in our ages would maybe be all right for a while, but not for very long. I find that I want to think long term. I'm not very good at temporary arrangements where men are concerned, that's what I've found.'

'Is that so?' he said quietly, looking at her intently with raised eyebrows in such a way that her flush deepened. She might have been the sixteen-year-old who had first set eyes on him, so vulnerable did she feel at that moment.

'Yes, it is,' she said emphatically.

'And have you had much experience?'

'No, I haven't. John would like to marry me, I suspect, if you must know,' she said. 'He hasn't actually asked me, but as good as. But that's not likely to happen…although sometimes I think I'd like to be able to work part time to spend more time with Alec before he gets to the age when he doesn't want to spend time with me, before he gets into those teen years that I'm dreading.'

'Marriage isn't a way out, Nell.' Joel said. 'Sometimes it can create more trouble than it solves.'

'How do you know?'

'I haven't been going around with my eyes and ears closed,' he said.

'I know,' she admitted. At the same time, she sensed that marriage to John would be very comfortable in many ways.

'I hope you'll tell me before you contemplate marrying someone…now that I've found I have a son,' Joel said. 'I know that I have no legal claim on him, but I would like to be part of his life and I think he wants me in his. I don't want any other man to take him away from me.'

'I thought you had stepped off the face of the earth,' she said, her emotions suddenly very much on the surface. 'For all I knew, you could have been dead.'

'Would you have cared?' he asked tersely.

'Yes, I would have,' she said, facing him. 'Shall we go on? I have some work to do.' She had almost been on the point of telling him that she loved him. It had also occurred to her over the last few weeks that she should propose marriage to him, if he would not do it himself, because she had an increasing sense that that was what she wanted, what would be best for all of them. Or maybe they could simply live together.

Joel took her arm and forced her to a halt. 'Can we at least agree on that point?' he asked, his expression tense. 'That you'll talk to me before you get into any relationship?' She did not see any affection there for her in his tense regard.

'If it matters that much to you, Joel,' she said, 'maybe we should meet to discuss this one weekend when we're both free. Come for supper, come for an afternoon, maybe on a Saturday, and we'll take Alec and the dogs for a walk through the ravines.'

'It matters,' he said. 'I'll contact you about it soon.'

'By the way, John does know I have a son,' she said carefully. 'They haven't met.

John's been very good to me, giving me time off when I want it to be with Alec.'

'Presumably he doesn't know about me and you?'

'No.'

Joel let go of her arm. 'I'll come to the floor with you,' he said. 'I have a couple of patients to see.' With a sigh, he thrust his hands into the pockets of his lab coat as he walked beside her, as though he could not trust himself to refrain from forcing her to make a promise.

Had she been surer of him, she would have told him then and there that no other man would be right for her, that he was what she wanted. As it was, it seemed that the ball was in his court and he would maybe never return it to her.

CHAPTER SIX

THE next two weeks were hectic at work. Nell was thrown together with Joel every day, in all the intensity and stress of the job they had to do, during which she saw and felt him watching her, as though he wanted to assess her, get to know her, in the shortest possible time. Subtly, he watched her with John.

With churning emotions, Nell realized, or thought she did, that Joel did not necessarily want her himself, but he didn't want anyone else to have her because she was the mother of his child.

They sweated over horrendous cases in the operating room, as well as the more routine ones, were on call together frequently at night for burns emergencies. They conferred about the best treatment for their patients, they spent coffee and tea breaks together. Very gradually she was getting to know the mature Joel, and he her.

Yet they were seldom alone with each other at work. What they did was very much a team effort. In many ways this supportive work ethos helped them to do what they had to do, yet as time went by Nell found that she was longing more and more to be alone with Joel, was aware of the tension building up in her to an almost unbearable degree, to get something sorted out between them.

So it was with relief that she responded to him one morning towards the end of the second week when they were momentarily alone at the scrub sinks in the operating suite, prior to their next case. 'We're both free this weekend, Nell,' he said, speaking hastily before they could be interrupted. 'How about if we make an effort to get together, with Alec as well?'

'That would be great,' she agreed. 'Spend the day with us on Saturday. Come for lunch and stay.'

Joel nodded, just as their privacy was invaded by other staff members coming to scrub for cases. A peace of sorts came over Nell as she went through the motions of her job automatically. They were going to talk about what would be best for Alec, and maybe something would come out of it that was good for them too.

Nell slept late on Saturday, as did Alec, both needing the rest. The ingredients for a simple lunch had been bought the evening before, on her way home from work. Having got up at half past six to let the dogs out to the garden, then back in again, Nell went back to bed.

Later, she and Alec prepared lunch—three kinds of quiche and a large mixed salad, with a tangy hors d'oeuvre of sliced mango and sliced avocado with fresh lime juice poured over, which she knew from experience was very refreshing on a hot day. It was a beautiful day, so she planned to eat outside on the patio.

'I know I've asked you this before, several times,' she said carefully to Alec, 'how do you like having your real father in your life? I mean, what has changed in your feelings since you first knew he was here in Gresham?'

'Well…it's good,' he said, screwing up his face in concentration, striving to get the meaning right. 'It was something I wanted, and now it's happening. He's a nice person. I don't know what I would have done if he wasn't a nice person. I just wish…I wish we knew what we were going to do in the future…how it's going to work out. You know, whether we're going to be a proper family. It's a bit weird, waiting to see what's going to happen.'

'I know what you mean,' she said. 'I feel the same way. It's something we can't really rush. We've got to get to know each other, because we've got to get it right.'

'Yeah, I know,' he said, sounding very mature. 'Will you get married, do you think?'

He sounded so wistful and tentative that Nell gave him a quick hug and kiss.

'I don't know...I really don't know. It's what I hope for.'

When the door bell rang at twelve o'clock she was carrying cutlery and glasses outside. 'Will you go to the door, Alec?' she said, rather unnecessarily, as he was already running into the front hall.

'Mum! Mum!' He was back moments later. 'Dad's brought his cat in a basket. He's a special cat because he won't come unless you whistle "Good King Wenceslas".'

'What?'

Alec repeated what he had said.

'Oh, that's odd,' she said, smiling at the imagery and struck forcefully by his use of the word 'Dad'. That was the first time he had called Joel 'Dad'. He had said it as though he had hardly been aware that he had said it, which signified to her that he must have been thinking about Joel in that way for a while, not just in an abstract sense of knowing that Joel was his biological father.

It seemed strange to her, bringing with it a dissonance, a feeling of wanting to share her son with his father, and not wanting to at the same time.

Joel came through to the kitchen, carrying a large wicker basket that had a lattice door at one end through which they could see a large black cat with yellow eyes which was glaring out at them. Much to Alec's delight, the dogs barked at the cat and the cat in turn yowled and hissed in a most threatening manner.

'Hi, Nell.' Joel grinned at her and kissed her on the cheek. 'I thought Alec would like to see Felix again, and vice versa.' At that point, the cat gave out a particularly angry wail of protest as one of the dogs shoved her nose very close to the door of the basket, making them all laugh.

'I'm not so sure you're right there about the cat liking it,' Nell said.

'Bring him out on the patio, Dad,' Alec said excitedly. 'Maybe he would like to be outside.'

'Sure,' Joel said. 'We can't let him out of the basket, but I know he'd like to be outside. He hates living in my apartment, so the sooner I get a house with a garden the happier he's going to be. I may just leave him with my parents.' As Alec went out ahead of Joel, carrying the cat basket, Joel looked back at Nell and raised his eyebrows in silent comment about the new word 'Dad', while Nell raised hers in reply, saying nothing. Progress was being made.

'You've made a hit, bringing Felix here,' she said to Joel, as they both stood on the patio moments later, watching Alec staggering around the garden with the large wicker cat hamper, before finally putting it down under the shade of a tree, sheltered from the hot sun.

After lunch—during which Alec had chattered practically non-stop to Joel about school, his friends, his summer art camp that he was going to—they prepared to go for a long walk with the dogs. Felix was deposited in a secure room in the basement, together with a box of soil as a toilet, some food and water.

'Will he be lonely?' Alec asked Joel as they set out.

'I expect he will,' Joel said solemnly.

'When I get back, can I have him in my room for a while?'

'If your mum agrees,' Joel said.

Joel and Nell exchanged glances. This was the nearest they had come to feeling like parents together, supporting their son and each other.

After a very enjoyable and long walk, and an early supper of leftover quiche and baked potatoes, when Alec was ensconced in his room with the cat, the door firmly shut, Nell and Joel sat on the patio having a cool drink.

'We have a few things to talk about,' Joel said softly, 'and we may as well do that now, as I suspect that such interludes may be few and far between over the next weeks. Although I hope we can get into a habit of walking your dogs on the weekends that we're not on call.'

'Mmm,' she said, nodding her head. 'Over to you.'

'I want your assurance that you won't marry without discussing with me what my role is to be with Alec,' Joel said, sitting opposite her, apparently relaxed, yet she sensed a tension in him that was immediately echoed in her. 'I assume that you would anyway, but I want to hear you say it.' By that remark he apparently ruled out marriage for them as a couple with a cold finality. He had, after all, said so before.

Nell took a deep, tremulous breath. Now was the time to get everything out into the open. This moment was, she knew, a test of her maturity. There were to be no more half-truths and hesitations. There was no point.

'Joel…' She cleared her throat. 'Before I answer that question I…I want you to know that I love you, I would like to be with you. There isn't anyone else I want to be with, and it's not just because of Alec. I doubt that I could take anyone else seriously, especially now that you've come back into my life...' Her voice trailed off.

Joel was staring at her, squinting against the bright, early summer sun, his expression unreadable. 'I wouldn't say that I came back into your life exactly,' he drawled after a long moment, his reaction difficult to interpret. 'Not in the way you seem to mean. If you remember, I told you that I was planning to come back to Gresham to be close to my parents.'

'Well...yes, but...here we are, Joel,' she said hesitantly, her sang-froid deserting her in the face of his apparent unmoving calm. To her, he was once again rejecting her.

'Yes, indeed, here we are,' he said huskily, a slight smile softening his otherwise sober features. Nell got the impression that he was trying very hard to control that softness. 'Is that a marriage proposal?'

'If you like,' she said, hardly able to get the words out because her throat felt as though it had closed up from nerves. 'As I said, there isn't anybody else. I guess I've always loved you...'

He took so long to say anything that she began to feel sick with apprehension. This mature Joel was perhaps more than she could handle.

'I'm tempted,' he said slowly, 'but I find that I can't trust what you're saying. I don't want to allow myself to trust it.'

'That sounds rather like damning with faint praise,' she said. 'Even though the word "tempted" does have a certain air of optimism about it.' To uphold her composure, she attempted to tone down the complete seriousness of her proposal.

'It isn't that I don't trust you as a person, Nell...it's not that exactly,' he went on. 'Perhaps it's more to do with me than you—my inability to have faith, or something. I have been accused of being caustic and sarcastic. But there it is, Nell, there it is. I was idealistic and upright in my youth, so maybe it's a case of the higher one goes, the farther one falls...or something like that.'

'I...I know you said that you don't want to marry, ever,' Nell said, a note of something like desperation in her tone. 'We...we could live together...here, with Alec. Between us we have quite a large extended family.'

'That way,' he said cynically, 'I would have no legal rights over my son, any more than I would if we weren't living together.'

'You mean you wouldn't want to live with me? Is that it?' She felt absurd at having to keep her voice down when she wanted to shout at him, to rant and rave. 'I don't understand what you want.'

'I expect I would enjoy living with you, Nell,' he murmured. 'I always did enjoy sharing the same bed, for the short time that we did so. I just don't know at this moment.'

'Really?' she said hotly. 'You can't have it all ways, Joel. If you don't want marriage, or to live with me, what else is there?'

'Two people don't have to be married or live together to share a bed,' he remarked casually, as though the matter were not deadly serious. 'That would be fine by me, so long as I could see my son.'

Momentarily speechless, she gathered her defences.

'Would it?' she said, her voice tight. 'I'm sick and tired of you judging me for what I did when I was sixteen. I was terrified, I didn't have any other way out…' Another silence took hold while she fought her emotions.

'I'm not exactly judging you, Nell,' he said softly. 'It's just that I've found over the past few weeks that I've felt very disturbed, more than I ever suspected I would, about the fact that for ten years I didn't know I was a father,' Joel said.

He got up and walked to the edge of the patio, looking out over the shady garden, his hands in his trouser pockets. 'All those wasted years.'

Nell got up to stand near him. 'I understand,' she said desperately.

'I can't trust, you see,' he said quietly, matter-of-factly. 'And that is a prerequisite for what you're suggesting. I can't trust that you love me, as you say. I'm not blaming you for that. Perhaps that's a fault in me, less to do with you…perhaps nothing to do with you. I don't know.'

'Have there been…many other women?' Nell asked, glancing quickly at his profile, hardly able to get the words out because her throat felt tight.

'Two or three,' he said. 'Who meant anything, that is.'

Jealousy of those unknown women added to Nell's emotional turmoil and she felt slightly sick. 'What happened to them?'

'There didn't seem to be any future in the relationships…for either of us,' he said.

Nell was absolved from replying by the sudden appearance of Alec at the patio door.

'Dad!' he said excitedly. 'Felix has climbed up to the curtain rod in my room and won't come down. He went right up the curtains. Come and see.'

'Sounds like he's ready to go back into his basket,' Joel said.

'I was wondering if I should whistle "Good King Wenceslas",' Alec said, grinning, 'to make him come down.'

'It's worth a try,' Joel said. 'I'll come up in a few minutes. I'm just talking to your mother.'

'Were you arguing?' Alec asked, looking perceptively from one to the other.

'No! Yes...sort of,' Nell said.

'About me?' he said.

'Indirectly,' Joel said quickly, saving her from having to answer again. 'Your mother thinks we ought to live together, all three of us as a family.'

Alec's mouth dropped open, then before he could say anything, Joel put a hand on his shoulder, turned him round to face the door. 'Come on, son,' he said. 'Let's get that hyperactive cat down before he shreds your curtains.'

As they disappeared from view, Nell let out a couple of succinct expletives under her breath. It was clear from Alec's expression that he would like nothing more than for them to live together. Maybe that would have some influence.

Well, she had put her cards on the table and Joel had not picked them up. Now Alec had been drawn into the discussion too early. And she again felt that obscure jealousy at the easy camaraderie between father and son. Although it was something she had both wanted and dreamed about, the reality made her feel that she was somehow excluded. It depressed her.

As she thought about it, she knew intuitively that it was something like the poignant regret that Joel was feeling for the years gone by. Maybe he was right to be cautious—after all, she hadn't thought about feeling excluded. Perhaps that was what parenthood was all about. You shared your children, you didn't own them, and at some point they would go away from you. With luck, if you had been a good parent, they would come back as young adults and remain in your life.

'Welcome to reality,' she muttered to herself. It was the reality of having to share the son she loved so much and thought of as hers alone. Her own parents had always been there, so she did not include them in her proprietorial feelings. Would I feel somehow vindicated if there was friction between father and son? she asked herself.

Carefully, because her hands were shaking, she gathered the glasses together onto a tray. Sudden tears filled her eyes, as a deeper feeling of sadness assailed her. For her, the mood of the day had collapsed like a pricked balloon and she didn't know how she would get thought the early evening.

As she loaded the cups into the dishwasher, Joel came back out to the kitchen and took her arm, making her pause. His face was pale and tense. 'You didn't really answer my question about what the arrangement would be between me and Alec if you were to marry,' he said. 'Let's get that clear.'

'I'm not planning to marry,' she said abruptly.

'Let's assume you are,' he said.

'All right,' she said, straightening up and pushing strands of hair away from her hot face. 'I would, of course, out of courtesy, let you know what was happening, and you would still be Alec's father and have contact with him, but I don't think I have to—in any way, shape, or form—ask your permission about who I marry. If you don't want me, you as sure as hell are not going to get any say in the matter if someone else wants me.' Abruptly, she shook off his restraining hand. 'I hope that's perfectly clear.'

Nell was breathing hard, blinking to dissipate the tears, humiliated by having bared her soul to no avail.

'Dad!' Alec called from the front hall.

'Alec!' Nell called, with an authority that her son would dare not challenge. 'I want you to help me clear up before you do anything else.'

'All right, Mum,' he said quickly as he came into the kitchen, sensing her mood.

'I'm not bringing him up to be a loafer,' she said to Joel.

They all helped to clear up the kitchen, Nell and Joel relieved by the charming chatter of Alec, who continued to tell Joel about the details of his life, as though he had been bottling it all up for a long time, just waiting for his real father to give a listening ear.

'Are we really all going to live together here?' he asked abruptly, having made an obvious effort to get up his courage to ask, looking from one to the other.

'Well,' Nell said, when Joel declined to answer. 'He…your father doesn't want that. Anyway, it's early days yet, you've only just found each other.'

'Would you like that?' Joel asked quietly.

'Yes, I think so,' Alec said. 'I'm the only boy at my school who has never had a father. Some of the other kids' parents are divorced, but the fathers come to the school sometimes, they see them sometimes. The sports days are the worst…' His voice trailed off, as though he had perhaps said too much, which might seem like a criticism of his mother.

Nell and Joel sat in silence, suitably chastened.

'Of course, I love Grandad,' Alec qualified, 'but I've always wanted my real dad…'

'That's understandable, Alec,' Joel said. 'I'm going to be around from now on. We don't have to live together for that. If you'll invite me to your sports day, I'd love to come.'

'All right,' Alec said, grinning.

A poignant sadness was so strong in Nell that she thought she might burst into tears, so she got up from the table to plug in a kettle for coffee and get cups out of a cupboard, thinking of the old saying about chickens coming home to roost.

In her mind's eye she could see Alec as a baby, smiling his first smile at her…Alec at eighteen months running towards her on a beach, into her open arms, laughing with delight…Alec digging in sand, with the sparkling sea as a backdrop…Alec at four starting junior kindergarten, his eyes wide with both interest and apprehension at having to go into a new world on his own. All that without Joel. Yet he had been in her mind. She had not fully considered that he would have been in the mind of her son also.

'Would you like coffee, Joel?' she asked brightly, blinking back moisture from her eyes. She hadn't realized that in her new incarnation as Dr Montague she could be so tearful. At least she wasn't dead emotionally, hadn't grown hard, from all that she had to deal with professionally, which was something she dreaded. That was something to be thankful for. 'Or maybe a glass of port?'

Joel came over to her. 'Let me help,' he offered gently. 'That was a great meal, Nell. Thank you. And it's been a long time since anyone's offered me a glass of port so, if I may, I'll have both coffee and port.'

'Sure,' she said. 'It's a good vintage port that a grateful patient gave me. Alec, show your father where the port is, and the glasses.'

So it was with mixed feelings that she and Alec waved goodbye to Joel shortly before it was time for Alec to go to bed.

'Bye, Dad. It's been a great day,' Alec had said as Joel had left, hovering close to Joel, sorry to see him go.

'Yes, it has,' Joel had said, ruffling Alec's hair, the dark hair that was so like his own.

'Will you come back soon?' Alec had asked. 'And bring Felix.'

'I'll come whenever you invite me. Thanks again, Nell.' As he had kissed her on the cheek, he had touched her face briefly with his hand. 'See you both again very soon, I hope.'

Nell shut the door. 'I'll run a bath for you,' she said to her son.

CHAPTER SEVEN

WHEN Alec was in bed, Nell collapsed onto a sofa in the sitting room, a small glass of port in her hand. Only now that she was alone could she let her emotions come fully to the surface, let the muscles of her face crumple into an expression of grief that she had held in check for most of the evening.

It was a relief to let the silent tears ooze out of her eyes and run unwiped down her cheeks. She let them drip where they would. Sometimes it was good to cry. 'Have a good cry, you'll feel better,' her mother had often said in the distant past. Usually, in the present, she had to be strong for other people—there were few opportunities where she could fully express her emotions. At work, her skills and training acted as a buffer between her and her emotions, otherwise they would often overwhelm her. Thus, there was a great satisfaction in honing one's professional skills. There wasn't the same buffer to prepare her for Joel.

Leaning sideways, she put her cheek against a soft, down-filled sofa cushion, letting all the emotion into full consciousness. Not least of all the concerns she was mulling over was the one of how her revelations of today would affect her working relationship with Joel, if indeed it would. Perhaps he had been aware that she loved him, before she had stated it so baldly. There would, no doubt, be a wariness between them. From long experience, she was good at tuning out her private life while at work. It was a case of discipline and necessity, to be totally focussed on the job in hand.

It was good to be alone for a while, in the quiet of her own house, with nothing that she had to do. She moved her gaze slowly around the familiar room she loved, sparsely but tastefully furnished with old pieces, some given to her, some bought at auctions and semi-antique shops. On the mantelpiece above the open fireplace a clock ticked gently, a soothing sound, like the beating of a heart. The house was old, mellow and benign in its atmosphere, full of character and history. The sitting room had oak panelling and heavy oak doors. Other families had lived there, happy families, she always liked to think, over the last one hundred and fifty years or so. Sometimes when she was sad she imagined that the spirits of those people gathered round her to give her support and love.

She had a mortgage on the house, her parents having loaned her the down-payment for it. She was hoping to pay them back over the next few years. All her life she had been surrounded by consideration and love. It had not been a calculated love that expected returns, yet it had been clear to her that her parents expected her to make full, positive use of what was given to her. They did not want it all thrown back into their faces. In order to give to her and her two sisters they has made sacrifices, financial and otherwise, which had become a way of life for them.

That same care had been extended to her son. Where they had left off, she had taken over. The biggest regret had always been that Alec did not have a father. Now she knew that she wanted to include Joel in her life, wanted to bring him into the circle, wanted him to be happy with her and Alec. As far as it was possible within her power, she wanted to help Joel to find the basic happiness that she had always had, even with the turmoil of being a single parent. You made yourself happy, that was her firm belief, yet sometimes you were a victim of circumstance, when you had to look for ways out and have the courage to take them. Sometimes, through no fault of your own, fate dealt you a blow.

Joel had also had a privileged childhood, he and his brother, which had, she knew, been tempered by a strong—and rare in their society—sense of *noblesse oblige*, instilled by his parents, who were both lawyers. They, too, had been loving parents, although they had not spent as much time with their two sons as they would have liked.

Nell let her mind dwell for a few moments on another topic that she usually shied away from: that of more children. She wanted more children, if she could, perhaps two more. Because the possibility of it seemed more and more remote, she pushed it away.

As she slowly sipped the port, as the measured minutes ticked by, she examined all the regret of the past and came full circle to the present moment. She had less regret than many individuals of her age; she had been very fortunate, her life was good. By the time the glass was empty she knew that she had done the right things that day. Let the future bring what it may. She would play it by ear.

As though on some sort of cue, as though she had conjured up something by the intensity of her emotion and longing, the headlights of a car passed a swathe of light over the sitting-room window from the now dark evening. It illuminated the room momentarily, where the curtains were undrawn. From her position facing the large bay window she could see, in the light of a streetlamp, that the car was Joel's and had made the turn from the street into the driveway of the house. It came slowly to a stop, then the lights were extinguished.

Calmly, as though she were standing outside of herself, watching her own actions, she got up quickly to shut the kitchen door, where the dogs were in their beds. Already one of them was barking quietly, having picked up a sound.

'It's all right,' she said to them. 'Lie down.' They were good, alert watchdogs, always protecting her, and she loved them fiercely. 'Good girls!'

Shutting the door between the kitchen and the hall, she padded with bare feet to the front door to open it before Joel could ring the bell that would send the dogs into a cacophony of barking.

He was the first to speak as he came close to her, illuminated by the light over the front door. He looked pale and haggard.

'Hello, Nell,' he said quietly. 'I found that I couldn't let this day go by without talking to you again. May I come in?'

She nodded, slightly muzzy from the port she had drunk, then led him into the sitting room and shut the door quietly.

'What?' she said, turning to face him, forcing herself to stay calm when she wanted to throw herself into his arms.

'I've been boorish and I've come to apologize,' he said. 'It's been a wonderful day, largely your doing, and I did my best to spoil it, so I'm sorry, Nell. Once I got back to my apartment, I realized how unforgivable I'd been.'

Nell licked her dry lips, staring at him, a gradual sense of something like peace coming over her as they stood close. 'You said what you thought at the time,' she said, her voice sounding rusty. 'I respect you for that.' With a calmness that she did not feel, she added, 'Come and sit down. Will you have a drink?'

'No, no drink…thank you,' he said, sitting down on the capacious three-seater sofa that she had just vacated. He had always been very polite, something ingrained from childhood, she knew. Now she felt a nervous desire to laugh hysterically, when she sensed that they both really wanted to fall into each other's arms, live for the moment, let tomorrow bring what it would.

'Coffee, then?'

'No. Sit down here, Nell.' He patted the seat next to him. 'If you'll forgive me for inviting you to sit in your own house. Only if you want to.'

When she sat, he put an arm round her shoulders and pulled her against him.

'That's better. You know there's an old saying, something about not letting the sun go down on your anger,' he said. 'Well, the sun has gone down, but it's not the end of the day yet, so I decided to make amends, if I can.'

'All right,' she said, sitting rather stiffly, almost unbearably sensitized to the feel of his body against hers, acutely aware that she was not being very articulate, yet knowing that she had talked enough earlier in the day and now did not trust her ability to control her own labile emotions.

'Is Alec asleep?' he asked.

'Yes, he went out like a light,' she said, feeling more comfortable talking about her son while Joel was looking at her in the way that a full-blooded man would look at an attractive woman, their faces almost touching. That look was what she wanted, yet she was frightened that she might not be ready for the challenge.

Over the years, so much time had been given to work and study that she often had not known how to respond when overtures had been made to her, feeling always that she had been waiting for Joel. Here he was, within kissing distance, his arm warmly around her shoulders, gripping her firmly as though she might take flight.

'Good,' he said. 'It might be a little premature for him to find me here so late.' Nell noted the nuance, that it might be premature but was not necessarily ruled out for the future…or so she thought.

With that, he bent down and kissed her, tilting her face up to his with his free hand. The touch of his mouth on hers was like an electric force, and she shut her eyes, letting the sensations he was evoking drown out everything else. Passion flared between them, as it had always done.

In the recent past they had kissed, yet it had seemed to her then like shades of the people they had been in their early youth. Now, as his mouth moved firmly on hers, assured and demanding, Nell got a greater glimpse of the mature Joel Matheson, the one she did not know, the one who had grown away from her, the one she wanted to know in the future. The insight was exhilarating as she found herself responding. Here was the mature man, the one she didn't know whether she could cope with—hard, spare and unforgiving. Nervous and unsure, she nonetheless kissed him back. She could not help herself, even if she had wanted to.

With his free hand, Joel swung her legs up onto the sofa so that she was lying down, then he lay beside her, enfolding her in his arms, hugging her close. 'I've wanted to do this all day,' he said huskily.

'I would never have guessed,' she murmured, her mouth against his, her arms around him. Once again she had the feeling of having come home, could feel his smile rather than see it.

'Am I forgiven?' he asked. He kissed her neck, her cheeks, her mouth.

'I'm not sure,' she said. 'I'll think about it. Have you...have you changed your mind about anything?'

'Not essentially,' he said, after a hesitation. 'I just want you to know I'm going to keep an open mind and vow not to be so boorish in the future.'

Nell stiffened, her increasing physical desire for him vying with an innate caution not to make herself more vulnerable than she was already.

'I—' she began, then he cut her off by kissing her, a long, lingering kiss that left her aware of nothing else but him.

Joel unbuttoned her blouse and eased it off her shoulders, then unhooked her bra and slipped it off, while Nell lay there as though in a dream. The room, where she had not bothered to put on a light, was illuminated only by a faint glow of a streetlamp. All was quiet. The pleasantly warm air of the room played on the sensitive bare skin of her breasts.

As Joel's hand closed gently over her soft flesh, brushing over a nipple, she held her breath, before letting it out in an involuntary sigh. At the back of her mind was the niggling idea that he was going to seduce her for reasons of his own, perhaps to prove something, but she didn't care—it was what she wanted, too.

'Joel, Joel…' she whispered, stretching up to tangle her fingers in his hair, kissing him as he smoothed his palm over her.

Joel drew back, propped himself up on an elbow and looked down at her, his breathing deep and fast. As he smoothed her hair away from her forehead, he kissed her eyelids gently. 'I wanted to test what you said,' he declared quietly, 'that you loved me. Among other things. As cynical as I am, I don't believe these declarations easily.'

'You believe me now?'

'Mmm.'

Sensitized to him with every nerve in her body, she looked back at him steadily in the gloom. Although she desperately wanted to know how he felt about her, she was not going to ask. There was a fear that he did not love her, that he was simply reverting to the physical relationship that they had had before. Well, she could wait. That he wanted her was very evident.

Nell pulled him down to her. 'Come here,' she said.

His sigh of pleasure as his mouth claimed hers vindicated all that she had said that day.

'I'd like to take you to bed,' he said after a while, his voice soft and husky. 'Is that possible and practicable? I feel I'm going mad with wanting you so much.'

Nell sat up and fumblingly put on her blouse and buttoned it up. Inside she was trembling, her desire for him goaded by his barely controlled need of her.

Silently she stood up and held out a hand to him. Together they went up the wide, old staircase that creaked now and then. Her bedroom was not close to Alec's, and she had a lock on her door.

Inside, with the door locked, she turned to him, and he began to undress her, his hands shaking slightly, his breath laboured.

When there was nothing left to take off, he drew her to him and ran his hands over her, down over her back, her hips, while she closed her eyes and clung to him. 'Oh, Joel,' she whispered.

'Is this what you want?' he said.

'Yes.'

He lifted her up and put her on the bed, then undressed himself, leaving his clothes in a heap on the floor. In a moment he was lying beside her.

'As happy as I am to have a son,' he said, his mouth against her ear, 'I'm going to be more careful this time.' She could tell that he was laughing.

'I'm glad you said that—' she smiled back in the darkness '—because I'm not prepared for this.' Happiness and a rare contentment erased everything else from her mind.

'Not in any way?' he teased softly.

'Well,' she murmured, 'I've waited so long for you. I can hardly believe this is real.'

'It's real all right,' he said. 'Little Nell Montague, grown up, so that I don't have to feel guilty.'

'You…you felt guilty?'

'Sure. Guilty as hell. As soon as I knew you were sixteen,' he said.

'Sorry,' she whispered, running her hands over his warm skin. 'No more guilt, then. I love you.'

In answer he kissed her, wrapping both arms around her, drawing her close. But he did not say that he loved her.

When the first glimmer of dawn showed itself through the curtains, he got up and left.

CHAPTER EIGHT

IT WAS midsummer and the sun was blazing in all its customary glory for that time of the year, with the temperature in the high twenties. As Nell drove to work she was glad of the air-conditioned car, while enjoying every moment of summer away from work.

That day she would be taking part in outpatient clinics, to do follow-ups on some patients, working with the staff men. Then she had floor rounds to do. For part of the day she might be accompanied by a medical student or two, she reflected, although the students had finished their academic year, taken their exams, so that the ones who were still around had summer jobs at the hospital or were staying on voluntarily, learning at the same time. She would wait to see who turned up.

These days, with the memory of Joel's love-making on her mind most of the time in quiet moments, she felt herself going through the routines of her life with that always in the background. Since that time, they had not met again except at work, having been extremely busy, yet had vowed to meet for another walk with Alec and the dogs when they were both free, if emergencies permitted. Although they were not on call during the coming weekend, anyone on the team could be called in for an emergency if the on-call team could not cope.

With the coming of the good weather, accidents involving burns took on a new dimension. Instead of so many house fires, brought on by heating devices, burns in cars, boats and industrial accidents often came to the fore.

After Nell had parked her car in the multi-storey parking lot opposite the main entrance of the hospital, she walked briskly though the main rotating doors to the large lobby and reception desk, down past the small coffee-shop that was for staff and patients, down the wide corridor that would take her past the large staff cafeteria and to the bank of elevators for that particular building. She had to go up one floor to get to the outpatient department, but before that she wanted to see two patients on the burns unit who had been operated on earlier in the week, where she had assisted. There would be new orders to write on the charts.

As she approached the entrance to the cafeteria, three doctors came out, wearing white lab coats over green scrub suits, the ubiquitous uniform, and she saw that they were Joel, Trixie and Rex.

Rex was the first one to spot her as she came up to their level. 'Hi, Nell,' he greeted her. 'How are you? You're just the person we want to see. Have you got a few minutes to come up with us to see David Tranby, Joel's patient, the one you operated on with us?'

Nell glanced at her watch quickly. 'I think so. I was actually on my way up there myself.

Don't have a great deal of time. Hello, Joel. Hello, Trixie.'

'Hello, Nell,' Joel said, smiling.

'Hi,' Trixie said, something about her expression letting Nell know that she hoped all was well between her and Joel.

Rex took her arm as they pushed their way forward into the crowded elevator. 'It's a relief to see you, Nell,' he said quietly as they squeezed together into a corner. 'Trixie has verbal diarrhoea as usual, which I'm finding increasingly wearing. Compulsive talking is, I have often thought, a form of aggression.' He tempered his comment with a grin.

'Don't be hard on her,' Nell said, who liked the chatty Trixie. 'Deep down she's like all of us, looking for companionship, attention and affection.' Right at that moment, Joel and Trixie were in conversation, with Trixie doing most of the talking. Seeing the two colleagues together reminded Nell sharply that she did not have any claim on Joel.

'Mmm,' Rex said. 'Maybe John should take her on, although I rather fancy he wants you.'

Nell did not rise to that bait. 'No comment,' she said. 'Why don't you make a few moves to bring them together? I'm sure you could do it.'

'Maybe I will,' he said.

Trixie was very beautiful, Nell considered, with her striking colouring, her red hair and green eyes, her delicate skin. Twinges of jealousy niggled at her as she watched her with Joel. Perhaps he fancied her, Nell thought sourly, looking at them quickly and away again.

How could she bear it if she and Joel did not actually get together? The possibility was there.

Once out of the elevator and walking into the burns unit, Joel detached himself from Trixie and came up to her. 'I thought you and Rex might like to have a closer look at David Tranby,' he said smoothly. 'Some of the dressings are being changed now. He's doing very well, no infection so far. He's looking forward to being discharged, but I want to keep him in a bit longer.'

'I'd like to,' Nell said, taking pains to keep her voice neutral as they entered the nursing station in the unit. Their mutual physical awareness was always there between them, the overwhelming attraction, which she had decided to deal with by just accepting it and not altering her day-to-day behaviour in any way if she could help it. Since they had spent the night together, Joel looked at her with a new warmth in his eyes, which made her long for him all the more. Yet, inexplicably, he did not follow on with any definite moves towards her. Perhaps, she thought sadly, it had to do with that issue of trust.

Trixie detached herself from their little group and began to go through data on a computer to get the latest lab results on her patients, for tissue biopsies, blood tests, culture swabs to detect infection, electrolyte balances and so on.

A nurse handed Joel a few computer print-outs. 'This is the latest on Mr Tranby, Dr Matheson,' she said. 'There's a nurse in the room, taking the dressings off. Everything looks good.'

'Thanks,' Joel said, taking the papers.

The three of them went into a small ante-room, off the room where David Tranby was in isolation. As they covered up to protect their patient from any infection they might bring in, Nell was acutely aware of Joel and tried not to make eye contact too often, yet did not want it to be the other way, to be too obvious to Rex that she was doing so, that there were vibes between her and Joel. Being too nonchalant was a dead give-away. Better to be as natural as was possible in the circumstances. Resolutely, she pushed thoughts of her personal relationship with Joel out of her mind.

'I have been to see Mr Tranby a few times,' Nell said. 'He seems in good spirits. And he was off the ventilator after the operation.'

'Yes,' Joel agreed. 'The grafts have taken well and, as you know, I have done a few more since the initial operation.'

When they went into the room a nurse had already removed some of the dressings in readiness for them to view the areas of new skin underneath before she applied new dressings.

'Hello, Mr Tranby,' Joel said. 'How are you?'

'Pretty good,' their patient said, from where he was lying on the bed. 'Looking forward to going home.'

'Won't be too long now,' Joel said reassuringly. 'These grafts look very good, no sign of infection. You remember Dr Montague and Dr Talbot?'

'Oh, yes,' David Tranby said. 'Good morning.'

'Good morning.' Nell moved closer to the bed to inspect the grafts, which were certainly looking as though they had taken well. The transplanted skin was growing well over the raw areas that had been burned.

'It's looking great,' Rex said.

After a few minutes Nell had to leave in order to see other patients, being on a tight schedule that day. 'I'll see you again before you go home, Mr Tranby. It's great to see you doing so well,' she said.

'Thank you,' he said, smiling at her. 'I appreciate all that you've done for me.'

Taking off her gown in the anteroom, Nell acknowledged that this outcome made it all worthwhile—the exhaustion, the sacrifice, the single-mindedness of it. Sometimes when she felt near rock bottom after a particularly grueling operating list or some terrible emergency, she thought of these times and they lifted her spirits.

After seeing the two patients that she had to see, she hurried to the outpatient department to see post-op patients who had gone home and were coming back for checks.

The morning seemed to go by with great speed, and after a quick, nutritious lunch in the cafeteria, she was back at her desk again in a small room, when the telephone rang. It was the nurse from the unit front desk. 'Dr Montague,' she said, 'there's a call for you from the emergency department. Will you take it there? I would have dealt with it, except that they want to speak to you personally. There's been a fire in a factory in the west end, a lot of burns, and they're coming here by ambulance, some of them. The doctors in Emergency are trying to round up some staff people and residents from the burns unit to help make the initial assessments and to stand by in the operating rooms as usual.'

'OK, put it through,' Nell said. 'I guess I won't have time to finish off my patients here. Could you fit them in with someone else, Maggie? Preferably with Dr Lane.' She knew that John was there and would only be called away to an emergency when all the other available surgeons on the team had been mustered.

'Will do,' Maggie, agreed, 'if you could let me know when you have to depart. I'll put the call though.'

The nurse on the line was from the triage desk in the emergency department. 'Hi, Dr Montague,' she said. 'I'm glad I've found you. We're getting a number of burns patients, coming in by ambulance. Don't know exactly how many yet, because some will be going to University Hospital and maybe a few other places.'

There were not many hospitals in the city that had specialized burns units that could deal with major trauma, so they did not have a choice about how many injured people they took. 'What happened?' Nell asked tersely, knowing that for the remainder of the day and maybe the evening and half the night she would be in the operating room.

'There was an explosion at a synthetic rubber factory in the west end,' the nurse said. 'Apparently it was caused by the ignition of a dust cloud in a particular part of the factory, flammable stuff. Some workers have died, some have bad burns.'

'OK. Would you page me when you know the approximate time of arrival? Give me five minutes, if you can. I'll be ready,' Nell said.

'Sure. From what I know now, they could be here within the half-hour. I'm trying to get Dr Matheson and Dr Talbot as well.'

'You've let the burns operating rooms know, I assume?' Nell asked.

'Yes, they're going to free up at least four rooms.'

Nell hung up and dialled her mother's number. On days like this, that promised to be long, she would ask her mother to keep Alec at her house and let him sleep there for the night.

Having done that, she arranged with John to take her remaining patients, then went to the female doctors' locker room in the out-patient department and changed into a clean scrub suit and lab coat. Looking at her watch, assessing where the ambulances might be at that moment, she made her way to the emergency department.

'You don't need to page me because here I am,' she said to the triage nurse at the front desk, remembering with a certain fondness how she had worked there as a volunteer. At that moment it seemed like a million years away.

The nurse acknowledged her presence with a wave.

They could hear the screaming sound of ambulance sirens when they were still some way off. At that moment, Joel, Trixie and Rex came into the department, as well as Bill Currie. With him was the intern, Dr Sy Grant.

'Will you help me, Bill?' Nell asked. 'Or have you already been spoken for?'

'I'll work with you,' Bill said. They worked together well as a team.

With so many patients coming in, each experienced staff person would have to take a case, perhaps with only one other person helping.

John appeared in the department. 'Hi,' he greeted them. 'I'm going to finish off a few cases in Outpatients, then I'll go straight to the OR to get ready. I'll leave you guys to make the assessments. Who's working with whom in the operating rooms? Have you decided that yet?'

'I'm with Bill,' Nell said.

'Right. Trixie, you work with Rex,' John said. 'Joel, you'll get one of the general guys who have been contacted to help us out. Sy, you'll be with me.'

'All right, sir,' Sy replied.

'Sy, you stay here just long enough to see how the assessments are done, then you come on up to the operating room. The emergency doctors will do some of the preliminary work down here—IVs and maybe the intubations if necessary—then we'll carry on where they left off.'

'Right,' the intern said.

'Where do you want us?' Joel asked one of the emergency room doctors.

'We'll be putting the burns cases in trauma rooms one through four,' he said, pointing. 'If we get more than four patients initially, we'll have to double up.'

'OK,' Rex said, 'let's get ourselves organized here. Bill, since you're working with Nell in the OR, maybe you can stay with her here. Joel, how about if Sy is with you for now? You'll learn a thing or two, Sy.'

'Sure,' Joel said. 'We'll be here for a few minutes only, I assume, then dash up to the OR.'

'Yes. Trixie, you and I will take a room each, if that's all right with you,' Rex went on, assuming a leadership role, as Joel had not yet experienced a disaster plan in Gresham General.

'Ready and waiting,' Trixie said.

Three ambulances pulled up one behind the other at the main loading bay, at which time the burns team dispersed to the trauma rooms.

Nell and Bill stood back as a patient was unloaded quickly by two paramedics onto the bed of the room they were in. An emergency doctor, an anaesthetist and two nurses stood waiting.

'Burns to seventy per cent of the body,' one of the paramedics said. 'She's had morphine, oxygen. There was some smoke inhalation and possible inhalation of toxic gases—she's got the IV Ringer's lactate going. We had trouble getting an IV line in, on account of all the burns, so went into the subclavian.'

'Good,' the anaesthetist said, helping them to move the patient, taking note of the IV line that had been inserted just below the woman's neck, at the side.

The two paramedics, burly guys in their thirties, were breathing heavily from the exertion and speed with which they had had to respond to and deal with this crisis. 'We just put in an airway,' one of them explained, 'but haven't intubated because we're not sure about damage to the trachea. She's breathing OK but respiration's a little fast.'

'OK,' the anaesthetist said. 'You did a great job, by the look of it. Thank you.'

Nell gave Bill a meaningful look. 'Now we know what we're up against,' she said. 'Let's move in for a closer look.' This was going to be a challenging one, and she felt herself gearing up a few notches.

With the others, they helped to cut off the woman's clothing, what was removable. Synthetic fabrics often just melted and adhered to the tissues of the body. Mercifully, her face and neck had been spared, but the rubber soles of her shoes had melted and adhered to the bottoms of her feet.

Nell and Bill wielded a pair of scissors each and made their assessment. They would get out of the way of the emergency team soon and prepare in the OR. Everyone worked quickly, not speaking unless necessary. Each person knew what he or she had to do.

The anaesthetist intubated the patient carefully, using a thin bronchoscope through a nostril to see his way down the airway to assess the damage inflicted by inhaled smoke and gases before inserting the endotracheal tube.

'I'll remove most of this burnt-on clothing in the OR,' Nell said to the emergency doctor. 'We'll go up now to prepare for her arrival.' All that would have to be removed with the general debridement.

'OK,' he said. 'Thanks for your help. We'll do what we can here.'

After talking to the anaesthetist, Nell motioned to Bill and they left the room to hurry towards the elevators that would take them up to the operating suite.

'What a mess,' Bill said, shaking his head. 'Does anyone know how it happened?'

'A dust cloud of explosive material, I think.' She said. 'I don't know what triggered it. I guess the factory didn't have sufficient safety measures in place.'

'I hope they get prosecuted to the hilt,' he said.

As Nell and Bill started the scrub procedure in the scrub room off the operating rooms, Trixie came in to join them, followed after a few moments by Rex and Joel. For once, Trixie was silent.

They discussed the cases briefly, then went to their separate operating rooms. 'Good luck, Nell,' Joel said to her quietly before they separated. 'We may have to combine forces to finish up the last few cases. Otherwise, maybe I'll see you in the middle of the night, which is about the time we'll get finished.'

'I'll treat you to a drink in an all-night bar,' Nell said, half joking.

'I'll keep you to that,' he said. Over the last days they had been polite and friendly to each other, professional. Nell did not discern any change of attitude in him towards her personally, although she often caught him looking at her when they were in a room together, would look up and find his eyes on her.

Later on that evening it was as Joel had predicted, four of them—Joel, Rex, Bill and herself were working on one of the last two patients, while John, Trixie and Sy were working on the other.

They were more than halfway through, with Joel and Rex doing the skin grafts, while she and Bill did final excisions of burnt tissue.

Utterly exhausted, running on adrenaline and nervous energy, Nell dropped a knife that had become slippery with blood. As the knife slithered to the floor, she looked at it and said, 'Bugger! As my old English grandmother would say.'

'I always find "Damn and blast" more effective,' Joel said lightly, his perceptive grey eyes regarding her over the top of his mask.

Everyone laughed, and there was a relaxing of tension while they took a few moments to flex and stretch tired neck and shoulder muscles. They had taken turns to scrub out to get quick cups of coffee, yet the effect was wearing off again.

'Have you got another dermatome?' she asked the nurse. 'Please.'

'Sure, several of them. We allow for at least one of everything to be dropped.'

'I find "Damn, blast and set light to it" better,' Rex offered.

Again they all laughed, a very necessary letting go of the tension of concentration.

'I could up that,' Bill said.

'No, don't.' Rex said. 'I might die laughing, and where would you be without me?'

'Up the creek,' Nell said, flexing her arm muscles, preparing to use the new knife. She had forgotten the name of the patient; each case seemed to be blurring into the one that had gone before.

'Without a paddle,' Bill said.

At last it was all over. The evening shift nurses had gone home, to be replaced by those on the night shift. The operating rooms had taken on that hushed, spectral quality of the night hours.

Nell found herself staggering a little as she went out to the scrub sinks, having thrown her soiled gown, mask, hat and latex gloves into the appropriate bins.

Ah, it was good to splash icy cold water on her face repeatedly. She felt faint from hunger, hypoglycaemic, and knew that her face was pale and drawn with fatigue.

John came into the room and put a hand on her shoulder. 'Are you OK, Nell?' he asked with concern.

'Essentially, yes. I'll be better when I've had something to eat and drink.'

At that moment Joel and Rex came in and Nell was surprised by the sharp look that Joel gave her, with John's hand still on her shoulder. Surely he wasn't jealous? She was too tired to speculate further.

'Must go to check up on my patients in the recovery room,' she muttered, 'before making the final exit.'

In the recovery room she checked on the patients they had operated on earlier. One or two had been moved to the burns intensive care unit.

'How are they all doing?' she asked the nurse. Extra nursing staff had been brought in to deal with the emergency. 'How's Ida Rowley?' She named the woman she had operated on first.

'She's holding her own,' the nurse said. 'Blood pressure's a bit low. We're dealing with that.'

After doing a quick round of her patients, checking the monitors and the vital signs that they were recording, she said to the nurse, 'I'm going home to sleep now before I collapse. I'll be back in the morning, not too early, I hope. I've got my pager if you need me.'

'OK. Goodnight, Dr Montague.'

'Goodnight, and thanks.'

As she left, Joel came in. 'Wait for me in the main lobby,' he said, at which she nodded casually.

In a daze of tiredness she left the operating suite and made her way to the female doctors change room near the outpatient department, where she had a shower and shampooed her hair before changing into her casual clothes, feeling a little more refreshed.

Joel was already in the lobby when she went out there, sitting in a patient area with his feet up on a chair. A security guard manned a small booth by the large rotating doors. This area was quiet at night, the main activity being at the back of the hospital where the entrance to the emergency department was situated.

When she approached, Joel stood up slowly to greet her, taking in her appearance, her damp hair and scrubbed clean face, devoid of make-up. At the sight of him her heart gave a flip of recognition and something like happiness, she supposed.

She still hadn't got over the fact that here he was, in this city and this hospital again, actually working with her. Their love-making seemed like something she had fantasized about. Sometimes it seemed that one day she would wake up and find that it had all been a figment of her imagination and desires.

His hair was also damp, and he was casually dressed.

'You look about sixteen again,' he said.

'I wish,' she said. 'I'm not susceptible to flattery, especially when I feel about ninety years old.'

'If you were sixteen again, would you do anything differently?'

'I don't suppose I would,' she said.

'What awful cases those were,' he said. 'We won't forget those in a hurry.'

'No. The smell of burnt flesh always seems to cling to the inside of your nose,' she said. 'When I was first on the burns service I used to put a bit of Vick's VapoRub in each nostril, so that I was breathing in the scent of that instead.'

Joel smiled, taking her arm. 'Do you still do it?'

'Eventually my supply ran out and I didn't get around to buying a new jar,' she said, her spirits lifting as they made for the door.

Before leaving they checked out with the security guard, showing him their identity badges.

'Ah…fresh air. What ecstasy,' Nell said, taking a deep breath, once outside in the pleasant night air. 'I'd like to get something to eat before I collapse.'

'I know a place that's open most of the night,' Joel said. 'It's behind the art gallery.' They began to walk briskly towards the parking lot. 'I thought we could take my car.'

'Then I'll have to come all the way back here to get mine,' she said, stopping to look at him.

'Not if you spend the night with me,' he said quietly. 'I'm hoping you will. Then I can drive you to work in the morning, or home, if you wish. I plan to sleep in for a while.'

When he reached forward and pulled her into his arms in the deserted parking lot, she felt bemused. It was so good to be in his arms. The tiredness seemed to fall from her and she felt cherished. At times like this her mood would often be marred by the sudden sharp realization that Joel had not committed himself to her in any way, and that he did not seem to be in any hurry to do so. The poignancy of her love for him was almost unbearable at times.

Instinctively her arms went round him, holding him tightly against her. 'Oh, Joel,' she said, as he bent to kiss her. 'I'd like that, but I'd rather go to my place in case Alec wonders where I am. He's at my parents' place for the night.'

The kiss rendered her weak at the knees and she leaned on him as they made their way to his car. More than anything she wanted to lie in her comfortable bed again with his arms around her, in spite of knowing that he wanted a sexual relationship with her and nothing else…apart from having Alec in his life. At that moment she didn't care, would take what he was offering. Maybe then she could put all the awful sights she had seen that day out of her mind.

The café was small and cosy, a French bistro. They sat close together at a very small table and drank the delicious soup of the day from enormous bowls, with crusty bread on the side. There were four other people in the café, apart from one waiter and the chef-owner who beamed benignly on everyone who came and went.

'I love this place,' Nell said to Joel. 'How come I've never seen it before?'

'It's very small, easily missed when you're walking by, behind the trees and shrubs,' he said.

'As well as the wrought-iron fence,' she commented, looking around her at the framed antique French posters on the crimson-painted walls. 'Do you come here much?'

'A lot,' he said. 'If you like, you can come here a lot with me, too.'

'I like,' she said, 'especially now I know that it's open half the night.'

He put a hand over hers as it lay on the table. 'It's nice to talk about ordinary things,' he said. 'Not about burns, accidents, explosions…disease, and all that stuff. We can pretend we're artist, or poets, starving in a garret, only able to afford soup…living for our art.'

'Yes…' She smiled. 'Instead of living to save other people's lives and sometimes screwing up our own in the process. Maybe the angst of the artist is no less than ours.'

'It would be arrogant to assume otherwise, I guess,' Joel said.

'I'm going to be out of character for a starving artist and order a small brandy,' she said.

Joel laughed. 'My fatigue is already making me punch-drunk, but I may just join you in that,' he said, as though mulling it over carefully. 'Before we become artists for a while, I've been wanting to say for a long time that, having worked with you, I've come to respect and admire you as a surgeon and doctor. I hope I don't embarrass you by saying that?'

'No. Thank you.'

'I'm getting to know you. Although we did work together when you were a volunteer all those years ago, it was rather different,' he said.

Nell traced an invisible pattern on the tablecloth with the handle of a spoon. 'Does that mean you're beginning to trust me?' she asked.

'I don't know,' he said.

'You haven't changed, Joel,' she said quietly, 'I'm glad to say. You always were a good doctor.'

He inclined his head in acknowledgement. 'Thank you. Do you think I'm using you, wanting to sleep with you?' he asked softly.

'Sometimes I think that,' she said honestly, 'but that doesn't matter, because I'll be using you as well. There's nothing that would stop me spending the night with you right now.'

Joel grinned, just as the waiter came to ask them if they wanted anything else. 'We have very nice fruit flan,' he said, in heavily accented English. 'Made by our chef.'

'Lovely,' Nell said. 'I'll have some peach flan and a small brandy, please.'

'The same, please,' Joel said.

'Do you think that accent's genuine?' Nell whispered to Joel when the waiter had departed.

'Definitely fake,' he said. 'Having worked in Montreal, I know a fake accent when I hear one.'

'Oh, really?' she said.

Joel leaned over and kissed her. As he did so, the awful images that they had seen that day receded further from her mind. They would come back, she knew, maybe later on in the night, when she might wake suddenly for no apparent reason and there they would be. This time Joel would be there, in her arms…

The dessert and brandy were brought and served with great aplomb.

'This is definitely out of character for starving artists,' Nell said, as she polished off the flan in short order, with sips of brandy in between.

Joel stretched his arms above his head. 'Ah, bed!' he said. 'I can't wait.'

'You'll have to,' she said. 'I'd like to pay for this meal, since you're giving me the pleasure of your company for the remainder of the night.' She grinned at him and he grinned back wolfishly. 'Not exactly buying your services, of course, since you've already offered them.'

'All right,' he agreed, gesturing to the waiter for the bill. 'I'm not averse to being bought, by the right person. Give the guy a good tip. He's a sort of muse, you might say.'

'Mmm.'

'Going to bed with you will be right in character,' he said.

* * *

Later in the night, Nell did wake. But the images in her head were not as she had anticipated: they were of the crimson walls of the bistro instead of the red of blood; they were of antique posters of Biarritz, Paris, Brittany, Provence, of truffle pigs and truffle dogs…

And she had Joel's arms warmly around her. When she turned her head softly to one side, his face was there next to hers, with the quiet, even sound of his breathing. It all seemed like a dream and, contented, she drifted back to sleep…

CHAPTER NINE

LIFE was hectic over the next two weeks. Among the burns patients who had been in the explosion, three were very seriously ill, mainly because of the extent of their burns, from inhaled substances and from some infection developing in their wounds and grafts. Nell found herself spending long days and parts of nights at the hospital, functioning in a constant state of exhaustion. Every spare moment she spent with Alec.

One morning, early, she met Joel in the nursing station at the burns unit, where she was reviewing the charts on cases and the latest lab reports on the computers there.

'Good morning, Nell,' he said. 'I guess you're here bright and early for the same reason that I am.'

'Yes. I'm worried about Ida Rowley. She had some damage to her airway.'

'That's the one with the shoes baked on to her feet?' Joel asked, as he searched out his own charts.

'That's right. I'm worried about the feet, too. There wasn't much left of the soft tissue, and the muscles were damaged.' She didn't have to tell Joel that she was worried about gangrene, that they might have to amputate the feet.

'She's John's patient, isn't she?'

'Yes, although Bill and I operated on her initially,' she said. Because she and Bill were both residents-in-training, the patient was under the main care of a staff man, in this case, John Lane.

'I can give you an opinion if you want me to,' Joel offered, 'since I'm here and John isn't. When are the dressings going to be changed?'

'We're taking her to the OR this morning, to do it all under a general anaesthetic. We want to get extensive tissue biopsies,' Nell said, referring to biopsies that she would take from various parts of the patient's body to monitor infection. If infection was present, the microbiology lab would identify the particular strain of bacteria involved, then she could treat appropriately.

'Give me a shout when you're ready, if you want me to take a look,' Joel said. 'I'm taking one of my own cases to the OR this morning, too, for review of grafts.'

'Thanks.' She smiled. 'John should be here pretty soon.'

Joel gave her an odd look at the repeated use of John's name. 'Maybe one weekend soon, we'll get to take those dogs of yours for a walk again,' Joel said.

'Sure hope so,' she said. At work she felt somewhat stilted with Joel, as though their professional life and personal life had to be very separate. Perhaps it was just as well, as memories of their love-making crowded into her mind when she first set eyes on him at any time in the hospital, and were then quickly suppressed with an extreme effort.

Other doctors arrived at the nursing station, so Nell left to go about her business.

First thing was to see Ida Rowley, who was in an isolation room in the unit.

Although a tracheostomy on the woman had been closed up and the endotracheal tube removed so that she was not on a ventilator and was breathing on her own, she still required intermittent oxygen to be administered through a mask. Suitably gowned and gloved, Nell went to stand beside the bed.

'Hello, Mrs. Rowley,' she said, 'It's Dr Montague again. We'll be taking you to the operating room soon, as I explained yesterday. How are you feeling this morning?'

Ida, drowsy from painkilling drugs, shook her head slightly and mouthed something. For the most part she lay with her eyes closed, sleeping or under the influence of drugs, during the many position changes that the nurses had to perform to prevent swelling of the tissues, congestion of the lungs and undue pressure on any part of the body from simply being in a bed. The bed could be tilted in all directions. Her limbs had been splinted to keep them in the optimal position, to minimize deformity from contracture and scarring.

While in the room, Nell checked the monitors recording the vital signs, as well as the intravenous fluid that the patient was getting.

As Nell was leaving, a physiotherapist came in and they exchanged a few words. 'I'm exercising the joints,' the other woman explained. 'It's slow going. But she's doing all right.'

They conversed quietly for a few minutes, Nell reminding the physiotherapist that their patient was due to go to the operating room again.

Nell sighed as she removed her gown in the anteroom, very conscious of how fortunate she was to be healthy, fit, young, to have a son, a loving family and a man that she loved...even if he did not love her. That he liked her would have to do. What she needed was a holiday. An uninterrupted weekend would do for now. She went out to see her other patients, and came across Bill and Sy in the corridor. They waved to her. 'See you in the OR,' she called, and they responded with thumbs-up signs.

During the operation for review of grafts, Joel found time to come in to take a look at them when the dressings were off, before John came into the room. 'These two look as though they should be removed and redone,' he said, pointing to two areas, relatively small, where the donor skin appeared not to have taken very well. 'That's what I would do.'

'Yes, I was thinking that,' she said. 'I'm going to take biopsies from those areas.'

John came in then, and Joel left.

'Morning, Joel.'

'Morning, John. Another day in the trenches.'

'You said it.'

At last the day was over and Nell found herself in the coffee-lounge with a few other lost souls who were recuperating from a heavy work day before finding the energy to either go home or to go on to other duties. The homely room, with its scuffed low tables, ideal for propping up one's tired feet, its fake leather chairs, its dog-eared newspapers and magazines, together with the kitchenette area, was likc a home away from home for those who landed up there at the end of the day. Tea and coffee always tasted so much better there than anywhere else.

Nell sipped from a large mug of tea and bit into an oversized doughnut, a once-in-a-while indulgence, while trying to catch up with the news at the same time by perusing one of the dog-eared newspapers. Some of the other surgeons came in, including Joel, who handed her a brown paper bag. 'A present for you,' he said very quietly. 'Open it later.'

'I already have a doughnut,' she said.

'It isn't a doughnut.'

Looking into the bag, she saw the distinctive green wrapping paper of an exclusive jewellery store enclosing a square box which was tied up with green ribbon. There was gold lettering on the paper, spelling 'Blanes', the name of the store.

When she looked at Joel with enquiring eyes, he avoided her glance, got himself tea and buried his head in a newspaper. She tried very hard to control what she felt was a rush of colour to her face. Perhaps, she thought, this was his way of asking her to marry him. Perhaps this was an engagement ring, although it felt rather heavy. With her heart beating fast, she left the coffee-lounge and made her way to the change room.

With hasty fingers she ripped the paper off, to reveal the distinctive box of Blanes, with its gold logo printed all over the cardboard. Inside the box was something wrapped in tissue paper, and a tiny card in an envelope. As she eased the object out of the box, it became clear that it was not the right shape for another box bearing an engagement ring. Carefully she removed the tissue paper to reveal a jar of Vick's VapoRub.

The little card read, 'Here is a new supply for you, with the memory of an enjoyable evening. It's great knowing you, Nell.'

With the jar in her hand, Nell began to laugh, going on until she felt weak. So much for the engagement ring. Was he trying to tell her something?

After putting the box in her locker, she decided to go back to the coffee-lounge to thank Joel for his present, only to find that the room was empty. 'Oh, well,' she sighed, 'I'll just have another mug of tea.'

Ah, it was so good to sit with your feet up when you had been on them all day, to cradle a mug of hot tea. All was quiet and peaceful. When she had drunk her tea she sat with her eyes closed, her head resting against the back of the chair, trying to empty her mind, to concentrate on her breathing in the way that she had been taught at a meditation class that she had taken some years ago. Very soon she would go home.

When the door opened about five minutes later, she did not immediately open her eyes, and when she did, she found John standing there in front of her with a look of concern on his face. So sure that it would have been

Joel, she just looked back at the man she considered her boss with a blank stare. As always, he looked trim and fit for a middle-aged man, with a head of thick iron-grey hair that, if anything, actually made him look more youthful than many men of his age. He had a thin, angular face and blue eyes, an attractive man, Nell considered yet again, dispassionately.

'Nell, are you all right?' John asked. 'You look very pale.'

'I feel pale,' she said, looking up at him, managing to dredge up a small smile. 'What a time it's been, eh, John? The last two weeks or so?'

'Mmm,' he said, seeming to her to be distracted, almost agitated. 'Once in a while we need something like that to keep us on our toes, to test our emergency protocol. Are you sure you're all right?'

'Apart from being able to use a weekend off, yes, I'm all right, John. How are you?'

He did not answer her question, went to pour himself some tea. Something was making him agitated, she sensed, and wondered if it had something to do with her, whether he had to tell her that she had made a less than optimal decision about a patient… something like that. Her intuition picked up something, a dissonance.

John put down his mug of tea on a table and sat down near her. Normally a man of quiet confidence, he seemed tongue-tied.

'Nell…' He leaned towards her, fixing her with an odd look that she had not seen before. 'This may not be the time or the place, but I have something to ask you that's been on my mind for a long time, and the opportunities to say it have been few.'

Oh, lord, she thought, have I not come up to his professional expectations, or something?

'The thing is,' he said, speaking slowly and with difficulty, 'I've been alone for a long time…and what I want to ask is…will you marry me?'

Nell stared at him blankly, her tiredness making her mind sluggish. Indeed this was not the time or place. It was something difficult to take in and she felt her lips part and her jaw drop in surprise. The look of stupefaction that she knew was on her face—although she was not really surprised—caused an answering change of expression in him.

'I...' she began, then tried again. 'I wasn't expecting this, John. I mean, not here and now.'

'No, I can see that,' he said quietly, in his usual somewhat dignified manner. 'I do love you, you know, Nell, so you must have had some idea.'

'Well, yes and no,' she said, desperately trying to think of something to say that would not sound inappropriate, wishy-washy or demeaning of him.

'I...hardly know what to say.'

'It obviously isn't a quick "yes",' he said with a rueful smile, which made Nell almost wish that she could love him, because he was a good man in every way. But the human heart was fickle and you could not force love, could not will it. Sadly, at that moment, she thought that maybe Joel had not asked her to marry him for the same reason.

'John,' she said, deciding not to prevaricate, 'I have to tell you, the father of my son has come back to live in Gresham, to be part of my son's life. I…I can't marry anyone else now…if ever.'

With admirable prescience, he said, 'Is he someone I know?'

'It's Joel Matheson,' she said. At last, in a very quick and unexpected way, the past seemed to have come to an end and a new era begun with the stating of the truth, bringing it into the open. The speed with which it had happened stunned her. 'I'm sorry, John. That's my position. I like and respect you tremendously. You've been wonderful to me.'

'But I'm too old for you and you love someone else,' he said, with only a trace of disappointment and hurt pride in his voice, a slightly stunned expression on his face which he seemed to be striving to control. 'I hope I haven't made too much of a fool of myself.'

'No, never that,' she said.

'I want to take care of you,' he said, very seriously, so that she felt a hysterical desire to laugh and then to cry.

'Sometimes it's very nice to be looked after,' she said sincerely, searching carefully for the right words, not wanting to hurt him, 'and, heaven knows, there have been times when I needed a partner to lean on. But now my days of needing, or expecting, to be looked after are over, John.' Strictly speaking, that wasn't true, of course. She was just as vulnerable as the next person, she knew in her heart of hearts.

He got up to stand in front of her. 'I can see that I have indeed chosen the wrong time and place,' he said. 'I'm sorry, Nell. It wasn't something I had planned before I came into the room just now. Seeing you sitting there, looking very pale and tired, with your eyes closed as though you might faint, I just came out with it—something I've been thinking about for a long time.'

Swallowing nervously, she stood up as well, feeling at a disadvantage sitting down. 'It's all right, John,' she said, surprised at how calm her voice sounded. 'I do understand.'

Abruptly the door opened and Joel came in, obviously perceiving instantly that there was an atmosphere in the room. Nell knew that her face was expressionless as she strove to control any obvious emotion. Joel said nothing, just looked at them, his eyes moving from one to the other, and simply raised his eyebrows in enquiry.

'I've just asked Nell to marry me and she's refused,' John said. 'You're the lucky one, I understand. Congratulations.' When he held out a hand to Joel, the latter took it automatically.

'Congrat—?' Joel began, his voice fading away. Her heart was hammering at great speed as she felt that events were getting away from her.

'I didn't say... We haven't...' she stumbled, addressing herself to John. 'Nothing has been decided.'

'You don't have to give an account of yourself, Nell,' John said. 'I fully understand. I was way out of line.'

'Don't apologize, please,' she said desperately, not wanting to see him inappropriately humbled.

As he made to leave, Nell said, 'Wait, John, please. Joel and I haven't exactly agreed to marry…'

'He's the father of your son,' John said, as though he had not heard her. 'It's understandable that you would want to be together.'

'Please,' she said, 'keep this confidential. No one else knows about us.'

'Of course I will…of course,' he said, ever the gentleman, and Nell's heart ached for him.

Then he was gone, leaving her and Joel to confront each other.

'What the hell's going on?' he asked, his face like thunder. 'What prompted him to ask you to marry him right here?' He looked pointedly around the scruffy, homely room. 'Or did you ask him?'

'No!'

'What, then?'

'Well, I didn't throw myself at him,' she said, getting back some of her innate courage. 'He thought I looked pale and fragile.'

'What?'

'Pale and fragile,' she repeated. 'He wants to take care of me.'

'Bloody hell,' he said. 'Now he thinks that we…that we are about to get married. Isn't that the gist of it?'

'Hole in one,' she said, getting furious at his incredulous expression.

'Don't be facetious. Did you lead him to believe that?' he went on furiously, frowning ominously.

'No, I did not. Repeat, *did not*,' she said, articulating each word forcefully. 'He made all the assumptions.'

'Before we know it, the whole place will be congratulating us,' he said bitingly. 'I'm not ready for that, as you well know, if I ever will be. I wouldn't put it past you to have engineered this.'

Without premeditation, Nell reached forward and slapped his face hard, the sound a sharp retort in the small, quiet room. What a relief that was! An awful silence ensued, into which her gasping breaths, as she fought for control of her emotions, intruded.

'Nothing was further from my mind,' she managed to get out through trembling lips. 'You really do think you're God's gift to women. It looks as though I've made a fool of myself with you, doesn't it?' she continued bitterly. 'I've been honest. You always were somewhat standoffish, Joel Matheson. You always put a high premium on yourself.'

'A high premium?' he said, frowning.

'Yes. It took you a hell of a long time to ask me out,' she said, 'when we worked together in the emergency department.'

'I wasn't exactly panting to get involved with someone, from what I remember,' he said bitingly. 'I was working like hell, had studying and exams to get through—I don't have to tell you that. You've been through it yourself. And you as sure as hell were not very mature, even had you been the nineteen that I took you for. You were cute, but so were a lot of other people.'

'John asked me because he loves me. He said so. That's more than you've said,' she went on. 'I assume you just want sex from me...now that you know how I feel about you.'

'He certainly made a hell of a lot of assumptions,' Joel said, ignoring the last part of her remark, putting a hand up to his face, which held a stunned expression and a red mark on the pale skin. 'Without any help from you, it seems.'

'We've known each other for a long time,' she said, mustering a surprising level of dignity. 'When I told you that I loved you it was because it was true, because I wanted to be with you. But know this, Joel Matheson, I'm not that desperate. I can take it or leave it. John's a good man, he'll keep his word.'

She moved round him and yanked open the door, while he stood glaring at her, his face paler than she'd ever seen it, his eyes dark and glittering with an unfathomable expression.

'That was the first time in my life that someone has asked me to marry him,' she said quietly. 'Not that I haven't had opportunities…it's more that I didn't allow myself to be in the way of a proposal because of what happened between you and me. I don't want to lay a guilt trip on you, it just happens to be the truth.'

'I can't help that,' he said.

With the door safely open and herself halfway through it, she turned back. 'Thanks for the Vicks,' she said. 'Don't bother to talk to me outside work unless you can say something civil, like an apology.'

'Wait!'

She almost ran down the corridor, which mercifully was empty as she could not control her features which she felt were crumbling into an expression of abject grief, sobs rising in her throat beyond her control. The first time in her life that she had had a marriage proposal…the reality was somewhat overwhelming, especially because it had happened at work. Sadly, it had been from the wrong man.

Seeing a woman's washroom, she quickly went inside and locked herself in a cubicle, letting the tears flow. She wanted to howl and sob, not having been aware of how close she was to some sort of breaking point.

No doubt she would be all right once she was home, had had a decent meal, a rest. When she had managed to control her feelings, she let herself out, washed her face and set off for the change room, hoping that she would not run into anyone she knew.

In the sanctuary of the change room she had a shower, taking her time. It would be a relief to get out of the hospital. There was a sense of mourning that the rapport she had built up with Joel had been shattered, plus the gradually developing feeling that he had played a trick on her by putting a jar of Vicks in a jeweller's box, duping her into thinking that it was an engagement ring, or at least a piece of jewellery. He must have known what she would think. What she had thought of as a joke earlier, she now thought of as thoughtless, even cruel.

When she came out of the change room Joel was waiting for her, lounging with apparent nonchalance against the opposite wall.

'I want to apologize,' he said immediately, straightening up, before she could get away. It was obvious to him that she had been crying, though she had washed her face twice. When she cried, her face always became blotchy and her eyelids swollen. He looked at her with a certain compassion that made her want to cry again.

'All right,' she said with a shrug, while a sobering sadness came over her. 'So much between us always seems to come too late, doesn't it, Joel? Like an apology. I feel totally washed out, and all talked out as well. There seems nothing more to say.'

For so long she had wanted to be with Joel, had fantasized about him, and now the reality was here, difficult to cope with, this hard, implacable man. Vaguely she wondered whether she was on the edge of a mental breakdown, after the years of being strong. The sadness she felt now was like a physical thing, weighing her down.

'Could we go out for a drink?' he suggested. 'There's something I want to talk to you about. It's important.'

'No,' she said wearily. 'I want to get home. I'm desperate to sleep, and I have to pick up Alec from my parents' place. I want to spend the evening with him.'

'Could I help?' he offered, as they walked to the entrance lobby. 'Could I pick up Alec for you, while you go on home and get something to eat?'

She shrugged, curiously emotionally dead, and she did not look at him. 'That would be all right,' she said in a monotone. 'I must get some food inside me. I'll call my mother to say you're coming.'

'Good,' he said. 'I'll see you before too long.'

Sitting in her car in the parking lot, she called her parents' place on her cellphone to let them know that Joel would be picking up Alec. It was a good thing she didn't have to go, as her mother would quiz her about looking upset.

Once at home, having petted the dogs and let them out, she headed straight for the kitchen work area, moving around automatically, in a daze. Something quick and easy was what she wanted, would make extra for Joel, as she knew he had not eaten, while Alec would have been fed by her mother.

All at once, everything seemed so complex, when she desperately wanted to simplify her life. From now on, she vowed, she wouldn't expect anything of Joel, she would just live from week to week as far as he was concerned. She would just get on with her life, as she had done before she had known that he would come into her life again. Yes, that was the way to go on, she decided as she searched the kitchen cupboards for that quick and easy meal that she had been thinking of.

A carton of organic vegetable soup came to hand and she tipped the contents into a saucepan, then took a salad out of the fridge that she had made the day before and beat up some eggs for two omelettes. Cooking was always relaxing, she found, as was the pleasant silence of the house and the totally accepting love of her two dogs, who were now looking at her with adoring eyes, their tails gently waving in anticipation.

'Yes, I am going to feed you,' she said indulgently, fancying that they could tune in to her depressed mood and were being extra gentle and patient with her.

They were incredibly sensitive to mood, picking up nuances of gesture and body language, tone of voice and so on. Cherry gave her an affectionate 'smarl', a sort of grin for which Dalmatians were famous, a drawing back of the lips, a wrinkling of the snout and baring of the teeth. In spite of her depression, Nell gave back an answering smile, a sense of peace tempering her mood.

'What would I do without you two?' she said. 'Food coming up.'

Alec hugged her when he came in, and she clung on to him, kissing him fiercely as though she had not seen him for a long time. 'Hi, Mum,' he said. 'I've had supper, and Dad has offered to help me with my homework.' He said 'Dad' in a very proud way, as though he was getting used to the word, and Nell felt an odd mixture of relief and despair.

'If that's all right with you, Nell?' Joel said, coming into the kitchen behind Alec. Although he seemed a little wary of her, the scene in the coffee-lounge might, apparently, never have happened.

She wondered what he was playing at, or was he just putting up a good front before Alec? Maybe he still didn't trust her. She wasn't so sure about his motives after the anger she had seen on his face at the hospital. Perhaps he thought she would try to keep Alec from him. If so, he didn't know her very well. Even though she might have twinges of jealousy, she would never do that. There was irony in the fact that she had taken pains to let Alec know, from a very early age, that he had a father, had spoken his name, had his photographs in the house.

She shrugged. 'If Alec needs help, that's fine…for a while,' she said. 'There's food.' She indicated the hot food on the stove and the salad on the kitchen table where she had laid two places, arranged so that she was not opposite him and did not have to look at him if she did not want to.

'Thank you very much. I appreciate it,' Joel said.

'I'm going upstairs to look up something on the computer,' Alec said to Joel, 'until you're ready.'

Nell and Joel ate in silence, an awful tension between them, which she wanted to break but did not know how. The hot soup was making her feel better physically. What she needed now was to sleep for at least twelve hours.

When they had finished their main meal and she had brought a bowl of fruit over to the table, she felt compelled to speak.

'It isn't going to work between us, is it?' she said quietly, so that Alec would not hear, that strange, sober, depressive feeling still on her, as though she would never laugh again. Perhaps it was the act of having struck Joel in the face that had somehow unhinged her—that, coupled with John's proposal. She wasn't sure. Joel's angry words had shocked her, too. All she knew at that moment was that she'd had enough.

'I don't know,' he said, 'to be honest. I have to talk to you. Maybe after Alec's in bed?'

Nell shrugged. 'All right,' she said. 'For the future, you and Alec can work out something between you about what you want to mean to each other,' she said, surprisingly making up her mind as the words came out. 'It doesn't have to be my decision. After all, he's old enough to have a say in how his own life is conducted.' It cost her something to say that, giving away some of the love and loyalty that her son had reserved just for her. 'I'm not one of those women who use a child to manipulate situations. I don't expect you to do that either.'

'I didn't think you were.'

'You surprise me.'

'What are your plans for a summer holiday?'

'We'll be going away to an island cabin with my parents—it belongs to them—just before Alec has to go back to school.'

'Nell…' Joel put a hand on her arm and she jerked away from him.

'Don't,' she said.

'Go and have a sleep,' he suggested. 'I'll clear up here, then help Alec with his homework. Then maybe we can talk.'

Leaving him to it, Nell went into the sitting room, shut the door and almost collapsed on the sofa. It was so good to lie down, to put her feet up, her head on a soft cushion. In spite of the turmoil in her mind, the sleep of exhaustion came over her almost instantly, a very welcome oblivion. As she drifted off, she acknowledged that it was good to have a partner in parenthood. If that was all she was going to get, so be it. From that moment she was giving up straining to find a way. The way would come to her eventually, or not at all.

CHAPTER TEN

A TOUCH on her shoulder woke her up.

'Alec's asleep.' Joel said, bending over her. 'Homework done.'

'Oh…' Nell sat up, smoothing her tangled hair away from her face.

'Thank you for doing that.'

'It's the least I could do,' he said.

Nell bit back a retort that he had done an about-face from his angry stance at the hospital. 'What do you have to say to me?' she said. 'We might as well talk here.'

Joel sat down at the other end of the sofa. 'What I have to say will give you the reason why I disappeared from your life all those years ago,' he said, leaning forward, letting his hands dangle between his knees, perhaps in an effort to force himself to relax. 'The reason I didn't tell you earlier is that I did not want to burden you, one, and, two, I didn't want you to feel sorry for me. Also, I wanted us to have a chance to get to know each other before what I have to say could come between us and influence anything.'

Again, that strange feeling of something like dread came to her, the feeling she had had when she had seen him at the conference, pale and tired.

'What is it?' she said.

'When I was doing burns training in Montreal,' he said, 'when we were still writing to each other, I became ill. Because of that illness, I decided it was time I stopped communicating with you, as there could not be any future for us. That's when I sent the Valentine card saying goodbye.'

Nell nodded.

'I had cancer,' he said abruptly, looking up to meet her eyes. 'I was diagnosed with testicular cancer.'

'Oh...' Nell put a hand up to her mouth, feeling as though her heart would stop. 'Oh, Joel, I'm so sorry.'

'To tell you the sequence of events,' he went on, speaking in a matter-of-fact way, 'I stored sperm in a sperm bank, then I had an operation to remove one of my testicles and some of the lymph nodes in the groin.'

'Oh,' she said. 'I never imagined anything like that. Perhaps I should have.'

'Why should you?' he said. 'We both had something to hide from each other. 'Ironic, isn't it? Maybe if we'd both been up-front from the beginning, things would have been better for both of us.'

'If I really had been nineteen,' she said, stunned and plunged into sadness by what he had said. 'I didn't dream…'

'Why should you have?' he said. 'Even though it's a disease of young men, it isn't something you necessarily think is going to happen to you, in the sense that you're looking out for it.'

'No…' Again, she wanted to weep.

'I decided to stop contact with you,' he went on, 'because I didn't want you to think

I was trying to have some sort of claim on you.'

Nell stared at him. 'That was the main reason I didn't tell you about the pregnancy,' she said. 'It's ironic, isn't it!' She got up to sit next to him, putting a hand over his. 'What a pair.' The anger, frustration and depressive sadness that she had felt earlier was somehow consolidating into a sense of bitter regret over wasted time. 'We could have helped each other.'

'I didn't want you to feel any sort of obligation to me. The last thing I wanted was for you to feel sorry for me…I dreaded seeing a look of pity in your eyes. You were so young. It was probable that what you felt for me would not last. You see, I would never have known whether you were with me because you wanted to be, or whether you pitied me.'

She squeezed his hand. 'I wouldn't have done that,' she said. 'After all, I told you a few lies because I desperately wanted to be with you.'

'Yeah, but for how long?' he said soberly, looking at her with keen eyes. 'I assumed that you would just grow up, would become immersed in your career and outgrow our relationship.'

That was, she acknowledged reluctantly, a fair and sensible assumption. 'That could have happened, but it didn't,' she said. 'I missed you like hell.' What an understatement that was!

'And now?' he asked. 'You said that you still love me, now that I look old, tired and sick. I wish I could trust that…not that it's necessarily going to make any difference.'

'I find that it doesn't make any difference to me—what you've just told me,' she said truthfully, still wanting to weep, his news like a physical blow. 'Are you…are you all right now?'

'I seem to be, so far,' he said. 'There hasn't been any recurrence. There was no tumour in the lymph nodes, thank God.'

'And the future?' she said, her voice tremulous. 'I don't know much about testicular tumours. I should, but I don't, other than what I learnt in medical school.' She felt sick, with an apprehension that made everything else that was happening in her life seem petty.

'With luck,' he said, 'there's apparently no reason why I shouldn't live out a full life span. On the other hand, this is a very difficult thing to live with. No one else can really understand…anyone who hasn't had their life threatened.'

'Joel…I wish I had known at the time,' she said brokenly. 'All those years.'

'I didn't want to burden you.'

'But it wouldn't have been a burden,' she protested.

'Yes it would have, at your young age,' he said. 'When you're diagnosed with a potentially fatal disease you go instantly into another world as soon as you're given the diagnosis…it takes seconds only. You go from the world of the well to the world of the unwell…and not just the ordinarily unwell. You go to a world where you can never take anything for granted again, not your life, your health or the surety of a future.'

They sat on the capacious sofa, holding hands. Nell swallowed several times to dispel the constriction of emotion that gripped her throat, fighting not to cry. Joel put an arm round her shoulders, pulling her against him.

'Meeting you again has been bitter-sweet,' he said. 'Not least because I often feel emotionally dead from the neck up. When you're told you have cancer you go into a parallel world, from where the door of the one you left behind will forever remain closed. That's the best analogy I can think of to describe it. If you had been older I might have told you. Friends, family, loved ones can't really understand, however much they care for you,' he went on, 'because it's something that you have to experience yourself to understand.'

'You make it sound so lonely,' she whispered.

'It is,' he said. 'For most of us, our own death is an abstract concept and, believe me, with this thing you feel the touch of your mortality. From the beginning, I've tried to guard against anything that smacks of self-pity.'

'I wish I had known,' she whispered, more to herself than to him.

'Hence the brush-off,' he said. 'I tried to do it in a civilized manner, so you didn't think I had anything against you. I hoped you would get the message from the Valentine card that I still loved you. My illness precluded any sense of permanence.'

'Don't say that. You're young.'

'Now I don't know what I feel. I can't pretend that it hasn't changed my life. Although I can still sire babies, so I've been told, I shall never marry. I couldn't lumber a woman with that…couldn't lumber you, Nell.' Although he spoke steadily, Nell detected an underlying bitterness.

'Why would it have to be like that?' she managed to say. 'If…if someone loved you, it would be all right.' He knew that she loved him, she had said so, with no qualification.

'Easy to say,' he said harshly. 'A woman would have to take on the burden of not knowing. I am quite contented with my life as it is. My work absorbs me. Having a son is an added bonus that I never expected.'

'What about us now?' she said.

'I don't know, Nell,' he said wearily. 'I don't know.'

'Do you love me?' she got up the courage to say.

'I don't know. All I know is that I'm jealous of John. I want to punch his teeth in when he looks at you as though he's some sort of predator and he wants to eat you.'

At any other time she might have laughed and maybe been flattered, but now all she felt was a sobering sense of dissonance.

'Maybe you'd be better off with John as a husband,' he said.

'No…never. It makes no difference to me, Joel.'

'I live from day to day. That's enough for now,' he said.

'How shall I tell Alec?' she asked, still wanting to weep.

'Don't tell him,' he said quickly. 'Please, don't tell him.'

Later, after Joel had gone home and she lay in bed with her eyes straining into the darkness, her mind felt as though it were a jumble of voices, all vying to be heard, a clamouring of discordant sound. Although she told herself time and time again that what they needed was to be kind to each other and have time to heal, a cold fear held her in its grip.

CHAPTER ELEVEN

OVER the next week, Ida Rowley passed a particular crisis point in that the fever that had spiked in her for a few days had been brought down by a course of a different broad-spectrum antibiotic, decided on according to results of tissue biopsies. Nell and John had had many consultations about her.

Nell was relieved to find that John's attitude to her had not changed. If anything, she detected an added gentleness in his stance. Perhaps, she speculated, Joel had recently told him about his diagnosis of cancer.

On Thursday the burns team, including the senior residents, held a conference about several of the more seriously ill patients who had been in the explosion at the synthetic rubber factory. Each staff member expressed an opinion about how each case should continue to be handled, in light of recent and ongoing developments.

These opinions were extremely useful, especially if a case was difficult to handle, with several possible approaches. While several more minor burns cases in the unit had been discharged home, those who had not been in the factory, there were several others who were going to be with them for a long time.

When the conference was over, Nell headed for the door, to be intercepted by John. 'Could I see you in my office for a few minutes, Nell?' he asked quietly.

'Sure,' she said, seeing out of the corner of her eye that Joel had paused and was watching them. His interest in what she was doing bothered her. It appeared that he did not feel there could be anything permanent for them, yet he did not want anyone else to be interested in her either, or so it seemed to her.

There was an incongruity in his attitude, even though she was striving to understand how he had arrived at that attitude, in light of his illness. After all, it had been years ago now. Now, with her new-found ability to withdraw, she just felt she could let it go, let it all flow over her. The sense of deep empathy that she felt for Joel fitted in with her new sober mood.

Over the past few days her mood had lifted a little, but not that much. Vaguely, she was aware that she seemed to have reached some sort of crisis point, at which past and present had come together in an explosive mix. The hectic pace at work had contributed to that.

Actually, in a perverse sort of way, she welcomed the depressed mood, because it somehow enabled her to withdraw, to stop straining after something that might never happen. It brought a relaxation of sorts, even though she was not exactly enjoying it, and enabled her to live in the moment. Whatever happened next, even if it was to be a non-happening, would have to come from Joel, because she was not going to take any sort of initiative. Already she had said all that she really needed to say.

If Joel wanted only a sexual relationship with her, then so be it, she had decided. He had his own reasons for not wanting more, while she loved him and would accept what he had to offer.

That decision was a great relief, because it seemed to her that she had spent the last ten years or so trying to put something right, as she saw it. Sometimes there was a peace to be found in living in the moment only.

Since Joel's revelation to her, they had reached a tolerable stalemate. They had walked together with Alec and the dogs, had managed to be pleasant to each other. What had not changed was their enjoyment in Alec, and Alec's obvious delight in the fact that he now had two parents. As time went by, she could see father and son becoming closer.

At work there was a gentle consideration in him towards her, which sometimes left her feeling tearful, so she would excuse herself quickly. Sometimes he would sit with her in the cafeteria and, apart from an acknowledging glance, she said nothing to him, could not think of anything to say that would not bring with it an unwelcome burst of emotion. She feared making a fool of herself in public. No doubt she would eventually get over it.

As head of department, John had an office in the unit, in a quiet side corridor. Once inside it, he shut the door firmly and got straight to the point.

'I've been talking to Joel,' he said. 'In fact, he approached me first, although I certainly wanted to talk to him. It seems that I got the wrong end of the stick, so to speak, about you two getting married, so I want to apologize again. He also told me that he'd had testicular cancer. That certainly puts a new complexion on things.'

They had been standing by the door, so he motioned her to sit down. 'You'll forgive me, I hope, for getting personal, but I do feel that I have a certain interest. Is there any chance that you could change your mind about us?'

'No,' she said, with her new-found courage, of which she did not know the origin, unless it was just that she had reached a point of not wanting to take more of the same. 'Whether there is any future for myself and Joel, we have more or less agreed to share parenthood of our son. It's about time Joel was in Alec's life. That's about all there is to it, John. Is this going to affect my or Joel's job?'

'No,' he said, and she believed him.

'You're going away on holiday in a few days' time, aren't you?' he said.

'Yes, I'm looking forward to it. When we get back, it will be time for Alec to start a new school year.' Nell stood up. 'I must go, John, I've got so much to do.'

'If I can help you in any way,' he said, 'don't hesitate.'

'Thank you.'

As she walked quickly away from his office, she interpreted his last remark as meaning that if she changed her mind about him he would be available.

The next few days were hectic, during which she concentrated wholly on her job. It was not possible to avoid Joel, of course, and they both were at pains to try to seem normal in front of their other colleagues. At home, she prepared for their holiday at her parents' country cabin on a lake. During her separation from Joel, she would have time to think. Before going away, she would have to take Alec to buy a new school uniform for the academic year, plus some textbooks, so that when they came back he would be more or less ready.

'Is Dad going to come on holiday with us?' Alec asked her one evening.

'No. He hasn't been in this job long enough to be able to take holiday time,' she said. 'I suppose he could if he really wanted to, but it isn't usual to do that. Maybe we can go somewhere hot in the winter, just the three of us.'

'Great!' he said.

It was with a sense of letting go that Nell and Alec drove out of the city a few days later, heading north and a little east, to go to the country where her parents' cottage was. Her parents had already left two days before with her two Dalmatians in the back of their station wagon. The separation from Joel was something that she both dreaded and welcomed—they both needed a respite from the heightened emotions that they experienced when together. No doubt she would, perversely, miss him intensely.

She drove automatically, not stopping until they were in a small country town and could stop for lunch. The temperature was in the high twenties, yet very soon there would be a quick change in climate and the cooling breezes of Indian summer would be upon them, fading into autumn, very welcome in the city. Already, it seemed to her a very long time ago that she had met up again with Joel and her life had been changed.

The time at the cottage went by very quickly, enjoyable and relaxing as always, even though both Nell and Alec missed Joel. 'I wish Dad was here,' Alec had said to her pensively on more than one occasion.

'He'll be waiting for us,' she said.

On the evening of the day they returned to the city, after she and Alec had eaten supper at home, out on the sunny back patio, there was a ring at the doorbell. A delivery man from a courier company stood there, holding a large object wrapped in Cellophane. 'Dr Montague?' he said.

'Yes.'

'These are for you,' he said, carefully proffering the object, as well as a smaller wrapped package. 'Would you sign for them?'

'Hold these, Alec,' she said to her son, who had followed her out, 'while I sign.'

In the kitchen they unwrapped the large package to find a terracotta bowl, simple in design, containing many exquisite red roses. As soon as the wrapper was off, their scent filled the room.

'Wow!' Alec said. 'There're one, two, three, four…' He counted the roses. 'Twenty-five! Wow! Are they from Dad?'

'I don't know,' she said, her fingers fumbling to open the small envelope containing a card, overwhelmed, in spite of herself, at the beauty of the roses. These were no supermarket roses.

When she opened the card there was a single word written on it in black ink, in Joel's handwriting, which said, 'Forgive?'

'Yes, it is from him,' she said, keeping her voice neutral. So far, her son did not know that there was any bad feeling between them, although he was sensitive to mood and maybe knew more than he let on.

'That must mean he loves you,' Alec said, with solemn authority, 'because red roses are for love.'

'Is that right?' she said, finding that she could smile at her son in the midst of the depression that had lingered since before her holiday, which had been too brief.

'Yeah, everyone knows that,' he said. 'What's the other thing?'

Nell turned her attention to a small box that was in a Blanes bag. 'I expect it's Vicks VapoRub,' she said.

'What, from Dad?'

'He has a weird sense of humour,' she said.

Carefully she tore off the wrapping and opened the box. Inside that was a velvet-covered box in a deep blue colour and when she opened it she gasped in surprise. 'Oh, how beautiful,' she breathed.

Nestled in dark blue velvet was a large and solid-looking, beautiful engraved and filigreed gold locket, with a chain. It was an oval, burnished as though it was an antique, which she suspected it was. The letter 'N' had been engraved on the front.

'Is that from Dad, too?' Alec was incredulous.

'I expect so, but there's no card with it.'

When she opened the locket, there was the answer to Alec's question, for the locket contained both a photograph of her when she had been sixteen and one of Joel when he had been twenty-four. At that time they had taken photographs of each other often, they had not been able to get enough images of each other.

He had cut these photographs from larger ones, just head and shoulders.

Nell swallowed a lump of emotion in her throat, wanting to cry again. If this was his way of saying sorry, he could not have chosen a nicer way, yet the underlying sadness persisted in her as she put the locket back in its velvet bed. She had as much to say sorry about as he did.

'Are you and Dad going to get married?' Alec asked perceptively.

'I don't know, Alec. We've got to get to know each other again. That takes time. And, as I've said to you before, if someone doesn't love you, you can't make them love you.'

Her son looked at her very seriously and chose to say nothing. Perhaps, she thought, he was frightened of what she might tell him.

When Alec went off to read in the room off the kitchen, Nell moved the bowl of roses to the centre of the kitchen table and sat looking at them. Even as she admired their beauty and mulled over what they could mean, she still felt that underlying depression that she knew had a lot to do with Joel and something also to do with the horrendous workload that she had taken on in recent weeks, the nature of the emergency cases that she had dealt with. A short holiday had done little to dissipate that. Usually they took a longer holiday in the winter.

Upstairs she ran a bath for herself, put in some musky-smelling bath salts, lit an incense stick and a few candles. Knowing, rather vaguely, that her mood was too low to be healthy, she also knew that she had to pamper and nurture herself for a while, something that she didn't do very often. The holiday had rested her body sufficiently, but not her mind. She closed her eyes and relaxed back in the pleasantly hot water until her cellphone, which she had on a stool beside the bath, rang.

'Hi, Nell,' Joel said.

'Hi.'

'Just got back from the lake?'

'Yes.'

'How was it?'

'Good. Not nearly long enough.'

'How are you?'

'I've been better.'

'Where are you?'

'I'm in the bath. Until you called, I was relaxing. Is there a problem at the hospital?' she asked, hearing and applauding the hint of impatience in her own voice. 'I'm not available officially until tomorrow.'

'No, nothing like that,' he said soothingly, after a moment or two of silence, in which she sensed that he was picturing her in the bath. 'I wish I could be there with you. I've missed you and Alec.'

'Oh, yeah?' she said, borrowing a phrase from Alec.

'You got my flowers?' he asked, a hint of humour in his tone.

'Yes, they're very beautiful, and the locket…lovely. Thank you.' What was he playing at?

'Nell, I want to woo you,' he said, as though in answer to her silent question. She was so surprised that she almost dropped her expensive cellphone into the water.

'Good luck to you,' she said.

At that, he actually laughed. 'At least, you're getting your sense of humour back.'

'Am I?' No doubt he wondered what she was playing at. Well, she would tell him. 'That's not humour, Joel, it's depression. I reckon I'm suffering from a severe case of burn-out, brought to a crisis point by over-work and your general attitude to me, the lack of trust, and all that, so don't be patronizing. Up to now, I wasn't aware that I needed wooing, as I'd more or less thrown myself at you. Well, maybe you're right, because from now on I'm giving up, to save my sanity. So you run the risk that it won't get you anywhere.'

'Nell, could I come to see you…now?'

'No.'

'Why not?'

'I did a lot of thinking while we were away. As I just said, I'm giving up…and it feels good.'

'I missed you,' he said again.

'I missed you…a lot. But so would I have missed my dogs if they hadn't been with us,' she said, wondering where the words were coming from.

'So I can't come over?'

'No.'

'Can't you say anything other than that?'

'How about "Goodbye"?' she said, and switched off the phone by the push of a button.

Nell slid down into the bath water so that it was up to her chin and closed her eyes. As she lay there she had to admit that his gesture with the flowers and locket was very sweet, somewhat out of character, as he was a practical and pragmatic person.

Fifteen minutes later he called back, just as she was drying herself. 'I'm going to come over there to see you,' he said, 'because I'm concerned that you're depressed.'

'No. If you come, I won't let you in.'

'Alec will let me in. I just spoke to him and he would like to see me, and I him,' he said smoothly.

'That's despicable.'

'I'm actually in my car on the street outside your house. I'm hoping you'll let me park in your driveway,' he said.

'No. Bugger off,' she said.

'As your old English granny used to say?'

'Precisely.'

'In that case, I'll walk. I'm part way along the driveway now, in any case, approaching your front door and… Ah, yes, Alec is just opening the door for me, as I asked him to, so that the dogs wouldn't bark.'

Nell put down her phone and ran out to the upper landing, clad in a large bath towel, her feet leaving wet splodges on the polished wood floor. 'Alec! Alec!' she shouted down the stairs. 'Don't let him in.'

It was too late. She heard Joel's voice in the hall, and then there he was, bounding up the stairs towards her. 'I must talk to you,' he said. 'Please.' There was no trace of the humour of moments before. 'I've been as worried as hell about you, especially as John said you seemed depressed, a bit odd, before you went away.'

'Oh, he did?' she retorted, clinging to the towel that threatened to slide off. 'I thought he was a bit odd.'

'Be serious, Nell,' he said, coming forward and putting his hands on her bare shoulders.

'I am…deadly serious,' she said, feeling, at his touch, tears gathering in her eyes again. 'I wish that I didn't have to be.' She knew that excessive and uncontrollable crying was a symptom of a nervous breakdown. She didn't think she was having one as she was competent at work, but maybe she wasn't far off.

'Don't,' he said gently. He led her into her bedroom and shut the door. Awkwardly she held onto her towel while he put his arms round her.

'What's Alec doing?' she mumbled, using one corner of the towel to scrub at her face.

'I suggested that he should get on with unpacking,' Joel said, 'and that I would help him with anything a bit later on.'

'Is this part of the wooing?' she said.

'I was very worried about you,' he said, choosing not to answer.

'That's nice,' she said flatly. 'I find that at this moment I don't care about anything very much, except my son.'

It was nice to be held by him. Not that she was going to let him know it, having already revealed to him all of herself.

'Mum! Mum!' Alec was calling up the stairs. 'Is Dad going to help me with stuff?'

'I'm coming,' Joel called back. 'Listen, Nell, I'd like to spend the night here if I may, in your spare room. I don't want to leave you alone.'

'I suppose you brought an overnight bag,' she said tartly.

'As a matter of fact, I did.'

'Please yourself,' she said.

Later, when Alec was in bed and the dogs asleep, Nell got into bed, after locking her bedroom door.

Over the next two weeks, Joel slept in her spare bedroom every night, during which time they were civil to each other and she told herself that she was living in sublime indifference. Funnily enough, she didn't really question why he wanted to be there, just accepted it. Alec was delighted at the unexpected male company and chatted non-stop at breakfast time, which was just as well, Nell thought, as she and Joel did not have to talk much. Sometimes she drove Alec to her parents' place after breakfast, from where her mother would drive him to school later, or sometimes Joel would drive him.

There was a certain soothing quality to his presence, especially as he helped with child-minding and cooking. It was often said that you didn't get to know someone until you had lived with them. Often when she was at home she found that she just wanted to sit, sometimes in the garden, and gaze into space, not doing anything, just thinking, or its opposite—trying to clear her mind of pressing thoughts. Sometimes she tried to meditate. Sometimes Joel would sit silently with her, or watch her from the kitchen window.

* * *

One day during an outpatient clinic there was a call from the emergency department for Nell. 'Shall I put it through to your office?' the unit receptionist asked.

Please,' she said. 'I hope it's not another factory explosion, or similar.' Her thoughts went to Ida Rowley, who was now up and about most of the time and learning to walk again on her damaged feet which they had managed to save.

'Dr Montague? This is one of the nurses in the emergency department. We have your son here. Don't be alarmed, it's nothing serious, but he's had an accident falling off a skateboard at school and he's here with his grandparents. It's mostly cuts, scrapes and grazes, but we're going to X-ray his arm because he says it's painful...maybe a sprained wrist. We'll do a skull X-ray as well, just to be on the safe side.'

'Oh, my God,' she said.

'Everything's under control, Dr Montague, so don't worry,' the nurse said soothingly. 'Can you come down? He's asking for you.'

'Yes, I'll be there right away,' she said, rising from her desk.

It took her only moments to arrange for one of the other doctors to take over her duties, then she was hurrying along a corridor towards the emergency department, which was on the same level but on the other side of the large building. As she walked, she strove to calm herself. As a mother, she had been fortunate that Alec had not so far been seriously ill or been in an accident, other than the usual scrapes. She hadn't even known he had a skateboard at school.

In the emergency department she saw her father, Dr Montague senior, who was standing in a corridor obviously looking out for her, as he waved. In his professional capacity as a GP he sometimes met his patients in the department when they needed hospital care and wanted him to be there as well. Otherwise, it was not his milieu.

'Hi, Dad,' she said. 'I'm very glad you're here. What happened? I didn't know he had a skateboard at school.'

'It belongs to another kid,' her father said, giving her a quick hug. 'He's more or less all right, but I though we ought to get him checked. The thing got out of control and he ran into a tree.'

'Did he hit his head?'

'Sort of. He hit the side of his face, but not what you could really call a head injury,' her father said matter-of-factly. 'He's getting a black eye, it may be a real shiner. They're getting his head X-rayed and his wrist. There's pain in the wrist, so it might be a sprain. Anyway, dear, here we are, and he's being very brave.'

When Nell entered the treatment cubicle where her son was lying on a stretcher, with his grandmother at his side, his face crumpled when he saw her and held out his arms to her. On seeing her, he knew that he could drop his brave front. 'Mum!' he said.

What a relief it was to enfold him in her arms and see he was apparently all right. 'It's all right, darling,' she said.

Then she hugged her mother. 'What would I do without you?' she said, knowing that her mother understood she was fully appreciated.

'I was wondering the same thing,' her mother said, with a smile.

A young doctor came in to announce that he had arranged for X-rays, which would be done there in the department. A nurse came in and started to clean up cuts and abrasions on various parts of Alec's body, while Nell held his hand.

'You tried to knock down a tree, I understand?' the nurse said, gently cleaning a graze just above an eyebrow. 'And you've got yourself a black eye.'

The clean-up job was going to take some time, as there were grazes on his knees and elbows as well.

'Mum,' Alec whispered to her, his voice wobbly with emotion as he tried not to wince at the pain, 'I want Dad.'

Nell stroked his hair. 'All right. I'll have to go out for a minute or two to call him on my cellphone. If he doesn't answer, I'll have him paged. OK?'

Alec nodded, letting go of her hand and taking his granny's hand.

In the corridor, she saw that her father had gone to sit down near the triage desk, so she went in the other direction to a quiet spot where she could call Joel on her cellphone, dialling his portable phone, which she knew he always carried with him unless he was operating.

'Joel, it's Nell,' she said, her voice trembling. 'I'm in Emergency.' Quickly she went on to tell him what had happened, ending up by saying, 'He's asking for you. He said…he said he wants his dad.'

'I'll be right down. I'm up on the unit, just finished rounds,' he said.

'Thanks,' she said.

When Joel arrived, Nell was back in the cubicle and able to witness how Alec's face brightened when he appeared. The boy seemed relieved, and with a perception that came from knowing her son well she realized that he was relieved that Joel would respond when called, would be in his mother's life at work, would support her. This was in addition to the fact that Joel was living temporarily at their house, which they had explained to him by saying that Nell needed help because of hectic times at work.

Alec had seemed to accept that explanation, or if he didn't, he was doing a good job of pretending that he did.

'Well, little guy,' Joel said, grinning, 'you sure know how to get attention. I just had a quick word with your grandfather and he told me all about it.'

Alec grinned sheepishly. Both Nell and Joel held his hands, which were now bandaged. They tried to keep out of the way of the nurse, who was now working on his knees.

'When I've finished the dressings,' the nurse explained to the assembled family, 'we'll just wheel him down the corridor for X-rays of the head and the right wrist.'

When that time came, Nell excused herself and said she was going out for some fresh air. In truth, she wanted a moment or two to herself to calm the emotions that had been stirred up by the feeling that her son was being taken away from her. It was stupid, she knew, because it was what she had wanted. But, then, she had assumed that she would also mean something to Joel, that he would want her, too. A different equation was sobering and thought-provoking.

Outside the entrance she stood in the sun, leaning against a wall and letting the warmth of it play on her face and closed eyelids. Even the polluted city air had a scent of early autumn in it, a cooling breeze tempering what was left of the summer heat.

'Nell.' Joel was standing there in front of her. 'He's going to be all right. They haven't taken the X-rays yet, but I'm pretty certain he doesn't have a head injury.'

Nell nodded, swaying forward instinctively so that he put his arms out to support her and they closed round her protectively.

'If anything happened to him I would go mad,' she said.

He put a hand up to her head and pulled it against his chest, cradling her, not caring if anyone they knew saw them. In response her arms went round his waist, over his white lab coat.

'We've got to talk to each other,' he said, his chin against the side of her head, as though he was shielding her. 'We've got to stop beating each other up emotionally.'

'Mmm.' Once again, she wanted to howl and sob. All the past was piling up on her.

'There's something I want to know. It can't wait,' he said. 'Is there a possibility that you and John could get together?'

'No,' she said wearily. 'I told him no, and I can tell you no.'

'When I told him that we hadn't exactly planned to marry,' Joel said, 'I could tell that he assumed he still had a chance with you…and there was nothing I could do about it, even though I *did* believe you when you said you wouldn't marry him. He could be very persistent, I think, and wear you down.'

'No,' she said.

'You told me he wanted to take care of you,' Joel said. 'Well, sometimes that sort of taking care can be taking over. Unless I'm misjudging him.'

'I don't know,' she mumbled. 'I haven't given it much thought, and I don't want to.'

'Are you going to forgive me?' he asked. 'For being overly defensive and boorish?'

'It's something I'll think about over the next little while,' she said. 'I haven't been myself just lately… Or maybe I've been more of my real self—I don't know. Right now I'm concentrating on Alec.'

He pulled back and looked at her, gripping her by the upper arms as though she would take flight. 'There were so many things in the way,' he muttered, as though talking to himself.

Nell said nothing, just took it all in to be processed mentally later. There was no hurry to do anything. Sufficient unto the day…or whatever.

They stood there together, with traffic going by on the street, people walking in and out of the emergency department, an ambulance coming into the unloading bay beside them, and they ignored it all. Their thoughts were acutely attuned to their son. He had looked small and somehow fragile on the large stretcher.

'I find I'm a little jealous that Alec likes you, asks for you,' she said after a while, her voice flat, 'even though I want you to love each other…it's what I've wanted all his life.'

'It's understandable,' Joel said gently, his arms still round her. 'It would be odd if you didn't care in that way. You've had him all to yourself. Your parents don't strike me as being possessive or interfering types. They just get on and do what has to be done.'

'They're not,' she said. 'I'm all talked out, Joel. Maybe in the past I tried too hard to explain everything…came on too strong and apparently demanding. I don't know. Now I find that I don't care, because my emotions are flat. Nature's way of protecting me, perhaps.'

'I'm not going to takc Alcc away from you,' he said, stroking her hair. 'You're the centre of his universe. I'm grateful to you for giving me a child, as I've said before.'

'All right. I'll keep you to that,' she whispered.

'May I continue to stay at your house? I think you both need me, and I'm discovering that it's good to be needed by someone other than my patients. I'm enjoying it.'

When she nodded, he kissed her on the forehead. 'Let's get back in there, shall we?' he said.

It had been a long and strange day, another apparent turning point in a journey that had, lately, brought a lot of turning points, Nell thought as she and Joel sat down to a simple meal in her kitchen that evening.

'Will you have a glass of wine?' he asked, having brought a bottle of white wine home with him and put it in the fridge to chill.

'Please,' she said. 'Just a small one. Thanks for bringing it.' She wasn't going to take anything for granted, anything as her due.

Tired as usual, she found that it was a pleasant kind of tiredness because there was an underlying strange sense of peace that came with not striving any more. She didn't think it odd that Joel was living in her house, apparently keeping an eye on her. For so long she had fantasized about living with him that the reality seemed somehow a matter of course. That he didn't want to marry her was something to be put off for future consideration.

Alec was asleep, under the influence of a mild sedative to control the pain of a sprained wrist and multiple grazes. There had been no obvious head injury, nothing that showed up on an X-ray, yet she and Alec had been taking turns to check the pupils of his eyes as an unequal size could indicate a haemorrhage in the brain, something which might not be picked up by an X-ray initially if there was just a very slow, steady ooze.

'I want to say something,' Joel said, sitting there looking darkly handsome as he had always done, his now longish hair slightly untidy, lines of strain etched on his face.

'When have I ever prevented you from talking?' she said acidly, feeling her sense of humour struggling to reassert itself. One of the first things to go when you were down was your sense of humour.

When he grinned at her across the narrow expanse of the table she was devastated, although she tried not to be. The fact of his illness, of what it had done to him, what it was doing to her, was between them.

'Being with you and Alec has been wonderful for me, so I want to thank you, Nell. It's great being part of a family, and with this accident that Alec's had I'm sure getting my priorities sorted out,' he said.

'It certainly helps to do that,' she said, with no inflection in her voice, staring ruminatively across the room.

'If anything happened to either of you,' he said, 'I would be devastated.'

Nell inclined her head politely in acknowledgement. She had recently read in a book on meditation that happiness was here, now, in this moment. One should not look for it in some mythical future. 'I'm trying to live in the here-and-now,' she said.

'With the illness that I've had,' he said, hesitating, 'I feel that I've eaten of the tree of knowledge, which has brought me into a different level of consciousness, and there's no way of getting back into the garden of Eden. That sounds pompous, maybe. It's the best way I can think of to put it right now.'

Nell sat clasping and unclasping her hands in her lap. 'I think I know what you mean,' she said stiffly, 'but I don't believe in the garden of Eden. Do you think that I live in such a place, Joel? All unconscious of anything that's real? You're still capable of parenthood, you're healthy at this moment, you have a child. That's more than a lot of people can say. Look at Ida Rowley. Her life has been utterly shattered, through no fault or action of hers. She's survived, yet nothing will ever be the same again for her. What happened to her will affect all her relationships, will affect everything that she does in her life from now on. Yet she's so grateful to be alive, so appreciative of the medical care she's had…so humble…she makes me feel ashamed somehow.'

'I know,' he said quietly.

'I know I don't have to tell you that,' she said. 'I don't want to preach.'

Joel got up to carry their dirty plates to the sink and to put the fruit salad on the table that he had helped to prepare. When he served her first and poured her a little more wine, she felt cared for and cosseted, something that had been rather rare in her life until recently when he had come to live with her, and to her alarm the feeling brought tears sharply to her eyes. Again, she thought that uncontrollable crying, or the frequent urge to cry, were signs of an impending breakdown…

'Are you all right, sweetheart?' he said gently.

'I feel so weary…so weary.' She spoke almost to herself.

Later, in her comfortable bed, with the dim bedside lamp still on, she tried to clear her mind of all that had happened that day, using the technique of imagining herself in a wood by the lake, near the family cabin. In her mind's eye she was walking along a woodland trail with Alec, and then Joel was with them too, and the two dogs gambolling ahead of them. So much for living in the moment. She smiled to herself and closed her eyes.

When the door slowly opened and then closed, her reverie was interrupted and she looked up to see Joel standing there, clad in a robe.

'Alec is still OK,' he said. 'Pulse good and steady. No signs of bleeding.' They had agreed that Joel would get up in the night, several times, to check on Alec.

'Good,' she said, staring up at him. 'Thanks.'

'You forgot to lock your door,' he said, pointing out the obvious, still standing there.

'How did you know it ought to be locked?' she asked, her eyes going over him, noting his damp hair from his shower, his bare feet, his broad shoulders...

'Because I've been trying it every night,' he said, with a small smile.

Against her better judgement, she smiled. 'Oh,' she said. 'That's sneaky.'

When his smile broadened she felt herself losing control, noting how attractive he was, remembering how he had been when she had first seen him, her heart beating faster with a deep, powerful rhythm. She had got into the habit of sleeping in his arms...

'You'd better go out, so that I can lock it,' she said.

He came to sit on her bed. 'I prefer to lock it myself, from the inside,' he said, taking her hand and bringing it to his lips.

'I don't know that I'm ready for the continuation of what we seem to have started,' she said truthfully, although every part of her was longing for him to hold her.

In reply, he slowly turned her hand over and kissed the palm, the gesture sending a sudden cascade of desire through her body.

'Your idea of wooing?' she murmured, gazing curiously at her arm as he kissed her wrist gently, moving his mouth higher to her elbow. Each nerve end tingled as he touched her with his warm lips.

'Mmm,' he said.

He kissed her all the way up to her shoulder, until he was lying beside her, leaning over her, propped up on an elbow. It was impossible, she found, not to respond to him when he smiled at her and stroked the hair away from her forehead as he had often done in the past, impossible not to respond to the desire and warmth in his eyes. 'That makes me feel very cared for,' she whispered.

'I love you, Nell Montague,' he said.

So that warmth in his eyes was love manifested, she thought.

'Since when?' she whispered.

'Since you were about sixteen,' he said. 'I didn't want to admit it, because I had written myself off, I guess, where love was concerned. Then when we were all with Alec today, I knew that I loved you, never wanted to be away from you, that I loved Alec too. I'm pretty fond of your parents as well.'

They smiled at each other, allowing time for what he had said to sink in.

'Are you sure?' she said, putting her hands on his shoulders, leaning forward to kiss him.

'I've never been surer of anything in my life,' he said. 'May I stay here with you?'

Without speaking, she moved over and flung back the covers so that he could get in bed beside her, which he did, after shedding his robe and dropping it on the floor without the slightest embarrassment in his nakedness. She loved his male beauty, his lack of false modesty, his lack of arrogance, even though she had accused him of it.

In his arms she rested her head on his shoulder. 'And I love you, Joel Matheson,' she whispered.

'Did you leave your door unlocked deliberately?' he murmured in her ear, kissing it.

'You mean, accidentally-on-purpose? As my—'

'Old granny used to say,' he finished for her.

As they both laughed, a feeling welled up in her that she recognized as joy…something she had not experienced properly for some time. 'To be honest, I don't know. Maybe it was a Freudian slip,' she said.

They held each other tightly. 'I've finally come home, Nell,' he said. 'If you'll have me.'

'What about your garden of Eden?' she said softly, drawing back to look him in the face, seeing love there and a certain humility, letting her know that he did not take anything for granted

'I rather suspect that my garden of Eden is with you,' he said. 'You haven't answered my question, Nell Montague. Will you have me?'

'Yes. Now...and always,' she said. 'You're my very best love.'

MEDICAL ROMANCE™

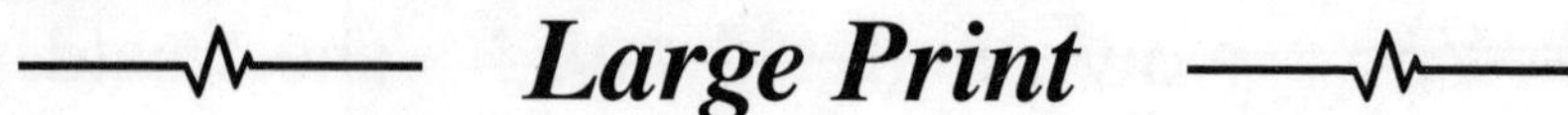

Large Print

Titles for the next six months…

December

IN DR DARLING'S CARE — Marion Lennox
A COURAGEOUS DOCTOR — Alison Roberts
THE BABY RESCUE — Jessica Matthews
THE CONSULTANT'S ACCIDENTAL BRIDE — Carol Marinelli

January

LIKE DOCTOR, LIKE SON — Josie Metcalfe
THE A&E CONSULTANT'S SECRET — Lilian Darcy
THE DOCTOR'S SPECIAL CHARM — Laura MacDonald
THE SPANISH CONSULTANT'S BABY — Kate Hardy

February

BUSHFIRE BRIDE — Marion Lennox
THE PREGNANT MIDWIFE — Fiona McArthur
RAPID RESPONSE — Jennifer Taylor
DOCTORS IN PARADISE — Meredith Webber

Live the emotion

1104 LP 2P P1 Medic

MEDICAL ROMANCE™

Large Print

March

THE BABY FROM NOWHERE	Caroline Anderson
THE PREGNANT REGISTRAR	Carol Marinelli
THE SURGEON'S MARRIAGE DEMAND	Maggie Kingsley
EMERGENCY MARRIAGE	Olivia Gates

April

DOCTOR AND PROTECTOR	Meredith Webber
DIAGNOSIS: AMNESIA	Lucy Clark
THE REGISTRAR'S CONVENIENT WIFE	Kate Hardy
THE SURGEON'S FAMILY WISH	Abigail Gordon

May

THE POLICE DOCTOR'S SECRET	Marion Lennox
THE RECOVERY ASSIGNMENT	Alison Roberts
ONE NIGHT IN EMERGENCY	Carol Marinelli
CARING FOR HIS BABIES	Lilian Darcy

Live the emotion

1104 LP 2P P2 Medical